D0408045

DISCARD

# The Castaways

## ALSO BY IAIN LAWRENCE

*The Cannibals*

*The Convicts*

*Gemini Summer*

*B for Buster*

*The Lightkeeper's Daughter*

*Lord of the Nutcracker Men*

*Ghost Boy*

The High Seas Trilogy
*The Wreckers*
*The Smugglers*
*The Buccaneers*

# The Castaways

IAIN LAWRENCE

Delacorte Press

Published by Delacorte Press
an imprint of Random House Children's Books
a division of Random House, Inc.
New York


www.randomhouse.com/teens

Educators and librarians, for a variety of teaching tools, visit us at
www.randomhouse.com/teachers

Library of Congress Cataloging-in-Publication Data
Lawrence, Iain.
The castaways / Iain Lawrence. — 1st ed.
p. cm.
Summary: Bad luck continues to follow Tom Tin and his mates as they find themselves aboard a ship that had been abandoned, are taught to be sailors by two black-hearted castaways they rescue, and sail to a Caribbean island where they make important new friends and enemies.
ISBN 978-0-385-73090-7 (trade) — ISBN 978-0-385-90112-3 (glb)
[1. Adventure and adventurers—Fiction. 2. Seafaring life—Fiction. 3. Slave trade—Fiction. 4. Survival—Fiction. 5. Fate and fatalism—Fiction. 6. Caribbean Islands—History—19th century—Fiction.] I. Title.
PZ7.L43545Cas 2007
[Fic]—dc22
2006101156

The text of this book is set in 12-point Times New Roman.

Printed in the United States of America

10 9 8 7 6 5 4 3

First Edition

*To Rick and Kim,*

*&*

*Jan and Goode*

# contents

# *one*
## ALL AT SEA

We steamed along below the stars, half a thousand miles from land. All I could see were the dim shapes of the boys, and the hulk of the engine in the middle of the boat. But up from the bow flew splashes of green, like emeralds sliced from the black sea. In our wake they lay scattered, swirled by the churning of our paddle wheel.

All night I listened to the chant of the steam engine, the *chuckatee-chickadee, chuckatee-chickadee* that shook every plank and every nail. When the sun came up behind us, our smoke hung over the sea like a greasy pennant streaming from the funnel, a tattered flag that could be seen for many miles. So Gaskin Boggis pulled the fire from its box, dousing each stick over the side with a hissing gout of steam.

Through eleven nights we'd bored through the blackness; through eleven days we'd drifted on a blazing sea. On this morning, our twelfth since we'd last seen land, it was Walter Weedle's turn to stand watch, to keep a lookout for the black sails of the Borneo pirates. As usual, he went grumbling to his place atop the dwindling pile of firewood.

"There's some what never take a turn," he said, with a dark look in my direction. "Should be turn and turnabout, that's what I say."

Only Midgely bothered to argue. "No one minds what you say, Walter Weedle. You can hop it, you can."

Weedle's clumsy feet knocked the logs askew. "There ain't no pirates. We ain't seen a pirate yet. Don't know why we have to stop at dawn."

"'Cause you're a half-wit," cried Midgely. In his blindness he was squinting toward the engine, mistaking its shape for Weedle. "Try steering by the sun, and you'll go in circles, you stupid. But the stars is like a compass, and that Southern Cross is the needle. Ain't that so, Tom?"

"Yes," I said.

"It's going to lead us home. Ain't it, Tom?"

"Of course," I said, as though I actually believed him. Midge thought the Southern Cross hung in the sky like a painted sign. He didn't know how strange and pale a thing it was, so hard to find that I wasn't certain I had ever really seen it. I feared we were already lost.

"Tell him about them other islands, Tom," said Midgely. "Tell him how the Cross will take us there." He rattled off their names again, the Cocos, the Chagos, the Mascarenes.

"We can't miss 'em, can we? We'll hop from one to the other like on skipping stones."

He was smiling now, proud as Punch of this notion of his. He had made it sound so simple that we'd all believed it was possible. We had tackled the oceans as only boys might dare to do, chasing the Southern Cross toward islands rich with food and firewood. But now, if we didn't find land within the week, we would have no water left to drink, no food to eat, no wood to burn.

The sea was too huge, the sun too hot. I felt like a candle melting away. Weedle and Boggis and Benjamin Penny were as brown as old figs, while poor Midgely—red and peeling—looked like a lobster boiled in his skin.

He was taking shelter now as the sun climbed over the bow. He tucked himself into the shade of a sea turtle's shell, the last remains of a beast we had slaughtered ten days before. It was nearly as long as Midge was tall, and the boy peered out from one end like the turtle itself.

His eyes were gray, almost covered by his drooping lids. It seemed at times he had no eyes, when all I could see were the darkened crescents below his lashes. But he still smiled in his cheerful fashion. "All's bob, Tom," he said. "We'll reach them islands tomorrow, I think."

I didn't understand how he could never lose hope. I felt like flinging myself down in the kicking tantrum of a child, screaming about the unfairness of it all. I was the owner of a fabulous jewel, of a wealth beyond imagining. I had only to get home to London to claim it. But the Fates, it seemed, would never allow me that.

As I settled down beside Midgely, my thoughts ran their endless circle, beginning—as always—with the notion that I was cursed by the Jolly Stone. I believed absolutely that it brought ruin to all who touched it, and I vowed that I would one day unearth the jewel from its London grave just to pass on the curse to Mr. Goodfellow. I imagined with great pleasure how his greedy eyes would glow when I put the stone into his butter-soft hands.

Then, as always, doubts leapt in to chase this thought. How could a simple stone, a thing of the earth, carry such unearthly power? Wasn't Mr. Goodfellow really to blame? It was he who had sent my father to debtors' prison, and me to the South Seas in the hold of a convict ship. Give the diamond to him? Hardly! I would keep the stone for myself, and use its wealth to crush the man like a cockroach.

But what if the Stone were cursed, I wondered; and round I went again.

I could sometimes spend hours thinking in circles. But today I had only begun when the boat suddenly rocked, and my head banged against its ribs. Benjamin Penny shouted, "Watch where you're going, you great oaf!" Gaskin Boggis was moving to his place beside the engine. That was where he always slept, nestled with the machinery. To him it must have been like a favorite old dog, a friend to be fed and watered by night, to be petted through the day.

I tried to find a bit of shade behind Midgely's turtle shell. But with each roll of the boat, sunlight flashed across my face.

I lay on planks that were, at most, an inch in thickness. On their other side was water so deep that it made me dizzy to think of it. What manner of things lurked down there?

With the engine silenced, I could hear the slop of water beneath the boat. My horrors paraded in my mind: man-eating fishes; serpents and leviathans; storm and tempest; and every man who'd ever drowned. Of them all, this last fear was my greatest. The splash against the planks became the thrashing of lost sailors swimming up behind us. Every scratch and tap of wood was the sound of their fingers feeling at the boat, and I dared not lift my head lest I see them reaching for the gunwale.

I pressed more closely to Midge. "Don't think of ghosts, Tom," he said. By then he knew my every thought. "Think about the Cape, Tom. Think about England. Every morning we're closer."

He was such a kindhearted fellow. He never complained, and he worried more for me than he did for himself.

"Think of this too. She's a good boat." Behind his turtle shell, Midge tapped the planks, giving me a dreadful start. "Solid as a rock, ain't she? No fear there."

Well, he'd never seen the boat, not properly. Once as pretty as a music box, it was crumbling around us now, shaking to pieces from the thump of the engine. Trembling nails had raised their heads from the wood, and then their shoulders, as though trying to make a run for it. Planks that had sparkled were weathered and cracked, and the boat was shedding its varnish like snakeskin.

"All's bob," said Midge again, with a gentle squeeze of my arm. "Tomorrow we'll see land."

Above us, Walter Weedle turned lazily toward the south.

The scar on his face was more livid than ever, an ugly streak on his sunburnt skin. I no longer worried that he would do me in as I slept. Weedle was cunning, but cowardly too, and it shamed me to think I had once been afraid of him.

"It's always me and Penny what has to be the lookout," he grumbled. "Never Tom, and never his *pet* there neither."

He cursed little Midge. But the absurdity of a blind boy being a lookout must have occurred even to Weedle, for he muttered again and turned away. "Guess I'll outlive him no matter what."

I wriggled myself between the wooden ribs. The planks were dark and wet beside me, leaking where they hadn't leaked before. The sea was coming in, drop by drop, and our boat was slowly giving up the ghost. I thought our plight could be no worse. But then Weedle cried out, "Look there!"

He was turned toward the north, pointing across the sea.

# *two*
## A FLOCK OF BIRDS

"Look," said Weedle again.

I rose slowly, fearful of what I might see. *If there's a sail, please let it be white,* I muttered. *Even if it's British, let it be white.* I would rather be captured and put back in irons than be taken by the black-sailed ships of the Borneo pirates.

Benjamin Penny and Boggis were standing, staring over the sea.

"Black as death," said Penny.

My heart pounded as I stood and turned to the north. It wasn't a ship at all that Weedle had seen. To me, it was even more frightful.

The sky seemed shredded, the world split open. Black

clouds tumbled over the horizon, thick and lightning-struck, as though great fires were boiling from the sea.

"What is it, Tom?" asked Midgely. He was pulling at my ragged trousers. "Is it pirates, Tom?"

"It's a storm," I said. "The storm to end all storms, I think."

It was terrifying to watch it coming, to feel its breaths grow stronger. First the air grew crisp and crackly, and lightning flashed on the water. Then the seas built higher and higher. The rumble of waves was like the booming of thunder.

For as long as we could we kept at work. We stowed away the firewood, our last bits of food and water. We adjusted the towing line to our pathetic raft of firewood logs. But soon the boat began to pitch and rock so violently that we couldn't stand upright. So we huddled in its bottom, and the rain came down, and the seas roared over the sides.

Half that day and all that night we rode the wild waves, drenched with seawater, bailing for our lives. The boat groaned and creaked; the tiller thrashed itself from side to side. Our logs became battering rams, pounding at the hull, and we had no choice but to cast them loose. They went cartwheeling into the blackness.

In the morning the winds began to ease, and by noon we saw the sun. The waves smoothed at their tops but stayed as high as ever, and we sledded from one to the next, rolling the boat to its gunwales. The motion, with the sun and the spray, pleased little Midgely, who sat up with his salt-covered face in a grin. But for me it was sickening, and I lay like a pudding in the warm seawater that surged through the bilge.

Gaskin Boggis lumbered back and forth through the boat, gathering bits of wood that had lodged themselves in the most unlikely places. More than half our supply had vanished, and what sticks were left were sodden. Boggis arranged them like fish at a fishmonger's, spreading them out to dry.

Benjamin Penny was the lookout. He crouched in the very bow, a horrible figurehead soaring like a witch over the high waves. But Gaskin was the first to see the birds.

"Pigeons," he said, pausing in his work. There was a thick piece of wood clamped in his fist. "Look, there's a hundred pigeons coming."

"There's no pigeons out at sea," said Weedle. "One big loon, that's all there is."

"Tell him, Tom," said Boggis.

He dropped his wood and hauled me up on my rubbery, seasick legs. All I saw was water, till we soared to the crest of a wave. Then, across the valleys of the ocean, a flock of birds came into sight. There was such a mass of wings and feathers that it seemed at first like a torn-away bit of the sea, a bubble of blue and gray.

We tipped over the wave and into the trough. I staggered, but Gaskin held me. Then up we went again, though my stomach seemed left behind, and over the crest came the birds. They were fat and short, their wings beating madly. The whistling sound of their feathers carried me home in my mind, and for an instant I was small again, standing hand in hand with my father in a London square besieged by pigeons. The memory was so strong that I smelled the wool of my father's peacoat and heard all the bustles of London. It made me overwhelmingly sad for a moment, with the thought of my father captured by cannibals, of me steaming away from him as fast as I could. It was hard to imagine that I was living up to the riddle of his last words: *"Do what's right by me, Tom. Do the handsome thing."*

Boggis held me tight, as my father had held me that day in London, and I watched the birds dashing through the sky.

In the bow, Benjamin Penny lifted his little webbed hands, as though he might touch the pigeons. Weedle snatched up a bit of wood and hurled it at the flock, and the birds veered to pass around it. There were *more* than a hundred, and they whistled by—now close at hand, now high above—as we tossed and fell on the waves.

"Them's pigeons!" cried Midgely, hearing their wings. In his excitement his voice was slurred. "Pigeonsh, sure enough!"

We had seen albatrosses, and the menacing skuas, riding the breezes on great wings that never flapped. To see the pigeons flogging the air in their furious hurry was a sight that thrilled us all. We watched them until the sea again was empty.

It took blind Midge to understand what the birds really meant. "They're heading for land," he said. "We've come to the islands, Tom, just like I said."

Well, I thought he must be right. The storm had blown the pigeons out to sea, and all we had to do was follow them back. Our need to find land was stronger than my fear of pirates. "Gaskin," I said. "Start the engine!"

The storm had drowned the little embers of our fire. It took the better part of an hour to coax new flames from our wetted wood, half an hour more to build up steam. But at last the engine hissed, and the pistons stretched, and off we went across the waves.

Our smoke plumed from the stack in gray and brown, a signal to any ship for miles around. But we kept the throttle open, and the paddle wheel thumped, and the boat shook from end to end. Water oozed through the seams of the planking; every nail quivered, but we steamed for the land as furiously as the pigeons.

Benjamin Penny stood in his place with the spray flying around him, and the boat sometimes plunged so deeply that he was up to his knees in water. But he was laughing, shouting out that we were saved.

Gaskin bustled back and forth, round and round the boat. The door to the firebox clanked open and shut as he stoked the flames inside. Our supply of wood shrank alarmingly, but there was no need to spare it now. Low clouds appeared ahead, white and soft like cotton, shimmering with the reflected light of solid land, of trees. Then, just before dark we sighted the first island. It was very distant, only a smudge of green and black, yet the most beautiful sight I had ever seen. In a world that had been only water, the appearance of land brought tears to my eyes.

"I told you, Tom," said Midgely. "Didn't I say we'd see the islands today?"

He had to shout, though he was right at my side. The engine was a roaring dragon that gnashed the wood to embers, spitting out smoke and fire. Billows of ash spewed from the funnel, drifting down onto our skin and our clothes and our hair.

Boggis held up a stick and shouted above the noise. "It's the last of it, Tom!"

I didn't know what he meant. "The last of what?" I said.

"The firewood. It's finished," said he.

I looked around the boat, surprised to see that every stick and log was gone. We had pushed too far, too fast.

"Burn the boat," I said.

He set to with our little axe. He chopped away the seats, the knees that held them, the varnished decks at stem and stern. It seemed a dreadful thing to do to a boat, to feed it to its own fire, but Boggis kept that engine running through the night, and the boat shrank as we pushed on. At dawn we could see a faint white line from surf on coral reefs.

A most horrible thought passed through my mind that moment, as the morning sun glowed in treetops, on verdant glades. What if, somehow, we had gone in a great circle, to return to the cannibal islands? Or what if the men who ate men lived there and here and everywhere?

I poked Midgely. "Are there savages?"

"On the *Mascarenes*?" he said, as though I'd asked if there were men on the moon. "They're British, Tom, them islands. But no one lives there."

I longed so badly to step ashore that I was leaning forward on my seat, urging the boat to go faster, the way a horseman urges a jumper to the fence. Then I had no seat to sit on, for Boggis came and smashed it away.

He fed the pieces to the fire. He hacked our long sculling oar into six lengths and shoved them one by one past the red-hot door of the firebox. He burned the wood chips that he'd made. He started on the gunwales.

Five miles from the island, we could see the palm trees swaying. We could see the water curling up to break against the coral, the bursts of spray that leapt and vanished. We stared at the gap in the reef that would take us into sheltered water. The lagoon behind it glowed white and silver from the sand on its bottom.

Three miles from the island, we could smell the earth and the trees. Boggis pried the topmost plank from the ribs of the boat. In his arms he held every scrap of wood that was left to burn. I eased the throttle so that he could keep the fire going.

But less than half a mile from the island, the engine stopped.

*three*

# WHAT MIDGELY SAW IN THE OFFING

It seemed the cruelest fate to come so close to land, and not be able to reach it. But the boat was then just a hollow shell, like a cracked-open egg. The ribs were higher than the planks, so that their ends stood up like rows of teeth, or like the bones of a rotting carcass.

All day we drifted there, in the thunder of the surf, so close to the reefs that we could see starfish and anemones. We might have tried swimming ashore, if not for the dreadful surf, and for the sharks that we feared were lurking nearby. We prayed that a current—or a favorable change in the wind—would carry us through the gap to the sheltered lagoon. Yet it was not to be; truly, I was cursed. We drifted back the way we'd come, too slowly to see any change moment by moment. But the boom of the surf grew fainter, the ghosts of leaping spray grew smaller, and the line of palms along the shore became again a smear of green. For three days we could see the island. It shrank to half its size, to a speck, and one morning we woke to find that it was gone.

A sense of loneliness came over me such as I had never felt. I clung to Midgely, for the empty sea put terror in my heart.

I remembered being a child, and watching rainwater rise in a small pool. I had squatted down beside it to study four black beetles that were clinging to a twig stuck upright in the mud. They had climbed higher as the water rose, until they were clambering in a panic over top of each other on the last quarter inch of twig. Then that tiny branch had sprung loose, becoming an ark for the beetles, who had to squirm their way aboard as it spun and rolled, all topsy-turvy. I remembered being both horrified and thrilled. I was not yet six years old, already afraid of water.

Now I was no better off than one of those beetles. Oh, I could think and dream, and wonder about things. But in the end we were just five beetles being carried away by water and wind.

Night by night, the Southern Cross rose higher in the sky. We were drifting south toward the frozen continent at the bottom of the world, the soulless, hopeless Terra Incognita. The sun rose and set, and rose and set, and soon we had no food to eat, no water to drink. Even the rust-filled drippings that we could draw from the boiler were of no use. Gaskin Boggis, long ago, had watered his engine from the sea.

It seemed at first there was one blessing from our shared

misery, and it pleased me to find that we were better than the beetles after all. No one argued, and we pulled together. The squalls that we dreaded brought rain that we needed, and all five of us took hold of Midgely's turtle shell to form a basin for the rain. From that we drank together, bending our heads to the pool. Even Benjamin Penny, who had surely never once lifted one of his webbed hands to help another, took to diving below the boat to feed us all. He saw fishes down there sometimes, but wasn't fast enough to catch one. Instead, he brought up sponges and long-necked barnacles that he plucked from the boat's weed-covered bottom. We developed a taste for the baby mussels in their blue-black shells.

But the fishings ended with the appearance of a great shark. It sliced its fin across the waves one day, then round and round the boat. It never drew away, except to come back in a mad rush straight toward us. Sometimes it thumped against the planks with its back or its tail, and then we all clung to the boat, shouting together.

"It's an omen," said Midgely. "Sharks, they smell death. That's what the sailors say. If a shark appears, a sailor's going to hop the twig."

White as a ghost, it swam slow circles around us. It was always there as we drifted steadily south.

At night we dreamed of food. We all did, as though sleep kept us as close together as we were through the days. I dreamed of muffins and pies, Midgely of lemonade ices. The pangs of hunger and thirst that greeted us all every morning became too much to bear. Boggis was the first to drink seawater.

It made him violently ill, and taught a lesson that was never forgotten by anyone—except little Midgely. He took to lapping up—like a cat—the pools of salt water that collected at the stringers and the bilge. It only made him thirsty; the more he drank, the more he craved.

Midgely kept his vile habit so secret that I thought it was the fever that made him shiver and shake. I came to believe that he was not long for the world, that he was dying from the heat and the misery. I did my best to keep him comfortable, but the nights grew colder and colder. We saw an iceberg to the south of us, as big as a castle, with a blue gleam in its center that made me think of my diamond. Poor Midgely hauled himself up the shattered side of the boat, though he had scarcely strength to move. He turned his blind eyes to the south and begged me to see the iceberg for him.

"It's beautiful," I said. My voice was hoarse; it pained me to speak. "It's white and shining. There's arches and spires."

"Like the pearly gates?" asked Midgely.

"Yes," I said. He seemed very close to heaven then, and he must have thought so himself. It was only the next morning that Midgely talked of drawing lots.

The sun was just rising, and there was a thin mist—like smoke—on the sea. Midge held my arm and whispered. "It's what sailors do," he said. "They draw lots, Tom. First to see who does the killing. Then they draw again to see who dies. The first fellow gives that second one a bash with the axe and rolls him over the side. That way there's no screaming. No fuss."

The very idea disturbed me. "Why would we do that?" I asked.

He whispered in my ear. "To save the others, Tom. There ain't enough food and water for five of us. But there might be enough for four."

"Only for a while," said I. "Then there would be enough for three. Then for two. Then—"

"But Tom," said Midge in a whisper. "If we don't do nothing we're *all* doomed."

"I'd rather be doomed," I said.

Midgely insisted. He raised his voice until Benjamin Penny woke and called out from the bow, "What's he talking about?"

"Never you mind," I said. "The fever's giving him mad ideas."

The boat was rocking, groaning, on the swells. There was water oozing through every seam. Midgely drew me close. "Listen, Tom," he said. "There's more."

I could feel his breath on my cheek. His fingers were icy cold.

"It's going to be *him,*" he whispered. "I know it, Tom. Like I said we'd see them islands, and we did? That's how I know. It's going to be Benjamin Penny who goes over the side."

"I don't care who it is," I said.

Penny snarled like a dog. "That blind little bum-sucker, what's he saying?"

"We can cook his goose, Tom." Midgely squeezed my arm with sadly little strength. "We can give him his gruel."

I thought it was the fever that had changed him. His drooping gray eyes gave him the look of an old man, and the seawater had addled his thoughts. I loved him dearly, yet hated what he was saying.

"You'll be the one to do him in," he said. "I know that too; I seen it. You'll be the one to do the killing, but it's Penny what's going to hop the twig. That's why the shark's here; it's waiting for him. You can do it, can't you, Tom?"

"No," I said. "Of course I can't." It made me furious that he was so unlike himself that he'd think I'd agree to murder.

"Then all of us will die," said he. "Me, I'll be the first. You know I ain't got much longer, Tom. And you know something else?" His dried, cracked lips became a smile. "Penny will be the last. That's funny, ain't it, Tom? Penny will be the last."

"Oh, Midge," I said. But it was probably true. Benjamin Penny had the cunning, and the cold-bloodedness, that would let him outlive us all.

No one was sleeping anymore. Now Weedle and Boggis, too, demanded to know what Midge and I were scheming. So I told them straight out, thinking it would end all thought of it. "Midge wants to draw lots," I said. "To see who's thrown overboard."

They said it was folly; they said it was madness. "He's off his nut!" cried Walter Weedle, and Penny said things that were worse. I was pleased by the reaction. Or at least I was until I saw Midgely's face. He looked utterly crestfallen, as though his last hope had been snatched away, and I wondered if we hadn't *all* gone mad.

We went back to our places, but that wasn't the end of it. Once planted in our minds, Midgely's idea grew like a poisonous weed. What else did we have to think about? Hour after hour we sat staring at each other in the rocking, rolling shell of our boat. Weedle and Penny muttered about it as our last supplies dwindled. The meals that we divided became almost impossible to measure. On the first day that we had no water, everything came to a head.

"Draw lots!" cried Weedle and Penny. "The time's come. Draw lots!" they cried, as the shark swam round and round. "Do it now," they said, and the sunlight flashed across their faces.

For the first time ever, Penny and Weedle and Midgely sided together, against me. "You're always the one for fair and square, Tom Tin," said Weedle. "Well, it's three against two, ain't it? We'll do it ourselves."

I didn't trust Penny or Weedle, so I fell in with the plan, praying to God that I would be forgiven for it. I even made the lots, tearing five strips from the ragged edge of my shirt. In one I tied a tiny knot, then held up the five for all to see, and each was the same length and the same width, and apart from the knot they were identical.

I crushed each strip into a ball, and wadded the five in my fist. All the while I knew that I had gone as far as I could go from my father's idea of "the handsome thing."

We gathered in the center of the boat, where the bilgewater sloshed and gurgled. Benjamin Penny came down from the bow, dragging himself over the ribs of the boat. Midgely knelt on my left, Boggis on my right.

I held out my fist full of cloth. "Who will do the killing?" I asked.

No one moved. Midgely said, "Don't call it killing. Call it saving, Tom. That's what it is."

"Call it whatever you like." My hand trembled from the mere weight of the scraps of cloth. "Who will choose first?"

"It don't matter who's first," said Weedle. "Everybody chooses, and nobody looks until we've all done it."

"But who will be *first*?" I asked again.

I thought that none of them would dare to be the first, that even Penny didn't have the nerve to go through with it. But no sooner had I spoken than a hand reached out.

It was Midgely's. He nearly fell forward in his eagerness, groping first for my arm, then following it down to my elbow, my wrist, and at last to my closed fingers. He pried them open. He snatched out a strip of cloth and clamped it to his chest.

In a burst the others followed, Weedle last, and I was left with only one piece of cloth in my fist. Boggis asked, "Do we look now?"

"It's Tom Tin!" cried Midgely, though no one had yet opened his hand, and he could see nothing but gray. "It's Tom who'll do the bashing, ain't it?"

We unrolled the bits of cloth, and they flapped from our fingers like miserable flags. I stared at my own—the one with a knot at the end—then looked up to see Weedle, wide-eyed, looking back.

Little Midge, proven right, was already holding out his lot, pushing it against my arm. "Now choose to see who buys it," he said. "Choose who snuffs it, Tom."

It made my skin crawl to see his eagerness, his pleasure in this dreadful business. It came to my mind that he hadn't asked for this to save himself, or me, or anyone, but only because he'd seen the end for Benjamin Penny. He was at last reaping vengeance for Penny's blinding of his eyes.

We performed the same ritual, though with four bits of

cloth this time. I dropped one into the bilge and squeezed the others in my hand. I felt relief—despite myself—to be spared from this second, more terrible drawing. But now my hand shook worse than ever, and there was much sideways looking, much dabbing of tongues on sunburnt lips.

Again Midgely was the first to choose, nearly spilling the pieces from my fist. The others followed more slowly, and so Midgely spoke before all the lots were chosen.

"It's Benjamin Penny!" he shouted in triumph. "Ain't it? It's you!" He was standing up. For the first time in three or four days he came to his feet. The boat was rocking, and he swayed with the motion. "I *seen* it was you. I seen it in a dream, Benjamin Penny!"

Well, Penny turned white. He looked around from face to face, then down at his hand that held the lot. Only he could see the cloth that was folded in the cup of his palm. Then an odd expression came to his face, and a small sound exploded from his mouth, almost like a laugh.

# *four*
# A SAIL APPEARS, AND THEN AN OMEN

"Do him in!" cried Midgely. His parched throat gave him a witch's cackle. "Use the axe, Tom. Do it now!"

Penny let the cloth fall from his hand. It fluttered down and landed on the water in the bilge. It was clear of knots from end to end. Penny was saved.

"I seen it coming. I seen it," said Midgely.

Boggis spread his strip apart. Walter Weedle opened his. Little Midgely, still standing, flapped the piece of shirttail from his fingers. He was holding the one that was knotted.

"I knew you was done for, Benjamin Penny," he said. "I seen it days ago."

All four unknotted bits of cloth were floating at my feet.

I picked them up and stared at them, wishing I could fit them back into my shirt and undo all we had done.

At last, Midgely's voice faded away. We heard water gurgling below the boat, slapping at the paddle wheel. The fin of the shark made a little slicing sound through the waves, and the turtle shell rocked with a gentle tapping on the ribs.

Very slowly, Midgely changed again to the sadly serious little boy. He frowned, then sighed, then lifted his lot to his blind eyes.

"It's me," he said with quiet wonder. "Ain't it, Tom? It's me." He ran the cloth through his fingers, and drew a little gasp when he felt the knot.

Penny laughed. He laughed long and hard, with sinful cruelty. Then he picked up the axe and held it out for me. "Do it now, Tom," he said, mimicking Midge. "Do him in!" And he laughed again.

"Shut up!" roared Boggis. To me he spoke softly. "I'm sorry, Tom. I don't think your father would be happy with how we turned out."

I shook my head. "He wouldn't."

"We never should have drawn them lots," said Boggis.

"But we did," said Weedle. "So kill him, Tom. It's time!"

"I won't. I can't." I stared at them all, each in turn. "Look, I'll take Midgely's place," I said. "I'll take his lot as mine."

Midge shouted, "No!" He groped out and took hold of my arm, as though he believed I was already trying to throw myself into the sea. "Please, Tom. We did it fair and proper, didn't we?"

I picked up the five lots and placed them in his hand, so

that he might know it all had been done properly, if not fairly. He bunched them together, not even feeling for the knot. "Let's do it now," he said. "Just give me a moment first."

The axe was passed from Penny to Weedle to me. I led Midgely to the bow. He laid himself down, on his side, with not so much as a whimper. I rubbed his arm, then ran my fingers through his hair as he spoke to me softly.

"It was supposed to be Penny," he said. "But I was too eager, weren't I? It's justice, Tom."

"Justice? Why, there's no justice here." I felt as though my heart had been torn away. "It's the curse, Midge. It's that dreadful diamond."

"No, it ain't that, Tom. Luck was never with me, that's all." He put his hand in mine. "I was never meant to inherit no earth."

Benjamin Penny came creeping forward. "You're wasting time," he said. "Bash his head or I'll do it myself."

"Get back!" I shouted. "He can take as long as he wants."

But Midgely squeezed my hand and said, "I'm ready now." He closed his eyes. "Quick, Tom. One clean blow so's I don't have to drown, and put me quick into the sea."

Midgely covered his eyes with his fingers. Underneath, he was squinting, waiting for the blow that would be his end. But I couldn't do it. For the first time in my life I cared more for another than I did for myself. I dropped the axe and crouched there, weeping.

"Do it!" screamed Benjamin Penny.

He lurched along the boat and took up the axe. His webbed fingers wrapped round the handle.

Gaskin Boggis came lumbering after him, shouting at

Penny to stop. He made the boat rock and plunge. "Give me the axe!" he shouted.

I threw myself down to shield poor Midge, willing to take the blow in his place.

But it never came. Boggis snatched the axe from Benjamin Penny and hurled it into the sea. "There's a ship!" he said. "There's a ship out there."

It was a long moment before I could raise myself to the shattered planks and look out where Boggis showed me. I saw masts and sun-bleached canvas, and the dark hull of a ship.

"You see?" said Boggis. "I told you."

The ship came slowly on a breeze that barely rippled the water. It was old and weather-beaten, the sails all akimbo, the rigging in shreds. If the weather hadn't been so fine and steady, I would have sworn the ship had only just emerged from a raging storm.

Benjamin Penny gazed out at the ship with a look that chilled my blood. In his eyes was bitterness and disappointment! He had known the ship was coming—I could see it plainly—and he'd clamored for Midgely's execution even as rescue was on the way.

But as far as Midgely knew, it was a miracle that had saved him. He clasped his hands and said a prayer before he asked me, "What does she look like, Tom?"

"Strange," I said.

Long ropes streamed from the masts and the yards. A great bowsprit held sail after sail, and not one of them properly set. The enormous square courses were drawn up at their corners, giving the ship the look of a haggard old woman holding her skirts clear from the water.

The ship veered to left and right with a rippling of canvas. The sails collapsed as it rounded up to the wind, and all the loose ropes—the sheets and braces—flogged the sails like the whips of a lion tamer. As though beaten and herded, the ship fell away and gathered speed again. At each turn it sailed away from us, but always tacked again, and drew steadily nearer.

There was no sound of a crew. No orders were shouted. There was no stamping of feet, no hauling of rope. The ship appeared deserted.

I described all this to Midgely, who listened with growing dread.

"She sounds like the *Flying Dutchman,*" said he.

I knew the story of that ship; I'd probably heard it straight from Midgely. But he told it again as he stared with his gray eyes.

"She's been out here for centuries," he said. "Sailing through the Southern Ocean, collecting sailors on her way. She plucks 'em from their boats, or hauls 'em dead from the sea. If you see her you're doomed, if you ain't already gone."

"An old wife's tale," said Weedle, with a nervous laugh.

"She'll be an East Indiaman," said Midgely.

I wouldn't have known an East Indiaman from a duck. But Midgely described it as though he could see it himself, clear as crystal. "A long bowsprit. Three masts and a high stern. Big topsails and gallants."

That he could see with his dead eyes the very thing in

front of us was more eerie than I could say. All the time it bore on, ever closer, as I tried to tell myself that there was too much solidness about it for a phantom.

Boggis looked toward me with a frown. Weedle turned to Penny. All five of us were standing now, in the wallowing shell of our boat.

When the ship was very close it turned once more. The sails slithered over rigging and spars. They filled with a volley of hollow rumbles, or flapped uselessly aback. The ship rolled with the change of the wind, and a ladder of rope spilled over the side, as though thrown by ghostly hands.

The huge bowsprit passed above us, and the shadows of the sails slid over the boat, each hiding the sun for a moment. The hull was spotted with rust from iron nails, and the seams were gaping open. As the ship rocked back, and a passing swell sent us falling beside it, I saw seaweed and worms covering the planks. I fancied there was a smell of death in the air that wafted from the deck.

Weedle and Penny were pushing each other in their hurry to reach out for the ship. Though I had welcomed the sight of it, I was not eager to get aboard.

Neither was Midgely. "It's the *Dutchman,* all right," he said. "Tom, let's take our chances in the boat. Stay with me, please."

But the sea surged down the dark hull of the *Dutchman,* and sent our boat soaring beside it. We rolled on the crest, then slammed hard against the planks. I heard a crack from our timbers, and a groan from the ship. Our boat fell away, only to rise again more quickly.

"Push us off!" I said. But it was too late. We crashed sideways into the ship with a shock that stove us in. Our planks snapped; the ribs bent and broke. The sea came boiling through the bottom.

I held Midgely by the collar as water filled the boat. It spluttered and burbled into the empty firebox; it covered the pistons and the hood for the paddle wheel. It rose up the side of the boiler as the huge ship went gliding past.

Weedle and Penny jumped for the ladder, forcing the boat even deeper. Boggis managed to grab the rope with one hand, and with the other he reached out to help me. I lunged forward and clutched his wrist, still holding on to Midgely, who was shouting at me, for he had no understanding of what had happened. Then our faithful little steamboat vanished into the ocean, and the five of us clung to the ladder like my childhood beetles to their stick.

Thirty yards away, the great shark that had followed us now slowly turned. Its fin came through the water with a spray feathering up on each side.

We found a strength I wouldn't have thought we still possessed. Benjamin Penny scrambled up the ladder with Weedle at his heels. Boggis tried to haul both me and Midgely, but the weight was too much even for him. "Go up!" I shouted, and let go of his wrist. I plunged with Midgely into the sea, bobbed up on the crest of a wave, and barely managed to grab the ladder as the ship went sailing past. I held on to the last inch of rope as it dragged us through the water.

Boggis was a big and clumsy fellow. He moved as slowly

as treacle. But neither Penny nor Weedle appeared again to help him, and I dangled there as he struggled on. The waves kept passing, so that the water covered me now to my knees, and now as high as my chest. The shark was coming faster, a plume of spray rising round its fin.

# *five*

## A MAN IN A CAPE

Boggis climbed the ladder and hooked an arm across the railing of the ship. He reached down and bellowed, "Take my hand." But I couldn't let go of the ladder and still hold on to Midgely.

The ship rolled slowly. The water fell away along its planks, baring my waist, baring my knees. The shark came twisting through the sea, thrashing with its tail, and I drew up my feet just in time. I heard the snap of its jaws. I felt a scraping against my legs as it turned for another attack.

The ship was already rolling us deeper, the sea slurping over barnacles and sponges. Boggis tumbled over the rail and reappeared a moment later, lying across it on his belly. He grabbed the ladder with both hands and hauled it up, rung by rung, the ladder and me and Midgely too. His muscles bulged, his eyes popped wide, but he hoisted away. As my fingers met the rail, Walter Weedle reached out and hauled me to the deck.

We all lay in a heap, with Boggis more exhausted than I'd ever seen him. He gasped for breath.

There was not a sailor in sight, nor any sign of a crew at all. It was an eerie thing to lie on that open deck, below the sails and the towering masts. My father's ship had been forever busy, like a small town sailing the sea, but here was only the sway of ropes and the flap of canvas, and the faint tolling of a bell that came in time with the ship's steady roll. From empty davits—where a boat had hung—now dangled useless ropes.

"It's creepy, ain't it?" said Weedle. "Where's the captain? Where's the crew?"

He was frightened, I could see. He had hauled me aboard for his own comfort, not for my safety, but still I thanked him for it. The word rather stuck in my throat, and when I blurted it out he didn't answer. He was peering up toward the high deck at the stern.

"I think there's a fellow up there," he said. "I think I seen him moving."

We heard again the toll of the bell. But now it came in three quick strokes, as though a hand were ringing the time.

"Someone go and look," said Penny.

We all went together, in a cluster, with Midgely stumbling behind me. After the wild pitching of our steamboat, the slow roll of a solid ship threw us off balance. We went crossways up and down the deck, reaching out for support.

In the center was the high-sided hatch to the hold. We rested there, leaning against it, none of us too eager to see who was steering this ghostly ship. Boggis sat atop the hatch, then quickly leapt off as though it were fiery hot.

"There's something inside there!" he said. "Listen to the breathing."

I could hear it plainly when I put my ear to the wood. A murmuring sort of sound came in waves and rushes. It *did* sound like breathing. But it reminded me more of another time and place.

Boggis loosened the lashings. He kicked the iron dogs from their catches, then put his back to the hatch cover and raised it half an inch.

The sound grew louder. It took me back to the cannibal islands, to a dark and empty hut. I had heard the same thing there, only to come face to face with a clutch of shrunken heads hanging above a fire. Now I knew exactly what would come rushing from the hold, but it was too late to warn Boggis.

Through the crack he'd made, up from below and past his hands, came hundreds and thousands of flies. They came in a solid mass, overwhelming us in a cloud of wings and bodies. Boggis threw the cover back, and it fell ajar across the sides. We saw the hold crammed full of coconuts and breadfruit that were rotting in the heat. It was no wonder that the ship carried such a stench along with it.

We left the hatch ajar and continued on toward the stern. The flies buzzed in a flurry around us, scattering up through the rigging and over the deck. When we reached the end of the waist, where a staircase rose to the poop deck, I told the others to wait. I took a breath and started up the steps.

"If it's the Dutchman," said Midgely, "he'll be wearing a cloak. His face will be like a skull. He'll have only bones for fingers, and . . ."

I didn't want to hear any more. I hurried to the higher deck. I found the helmsman at the wheel.

Despite the sun and heat, he was dressed in heavy oilskins, in a cape that hung stiffly from his shoulders. He was staring straight ahead, as though as blind as Midgely.

True enough, he was thin as a skeleton. He had a scraggly beard, and scraggly hair that blew about him like cobwebs. He wore the hideous look of a man who had barely survived the fever. I might have believed he was dead already, yet there he stood on his own pegs, steering a deserted ship.

His eyes didn't move, his head didn't turn, as I stepped around behind him. It seemed he hadn't moved in ages. But the ship's bell was mounted on the binnacle in front of him—and there was no one else who could have rung it.

Boggis came up the ladder. He trudged toward me, muttering half aloud. "I don't care at all for this," he said. "A hold full of coconuts and flies, no one aboard, and the ship breathing and—" He stopped in his tracks at the sight of the helmsman. "Cor! Is that the Dutchman, Tom?"

Gingerly, I reached out to touch the man's shoulder. I knew the fever might still lurk in his skin and his blood, and so was careful to touch only his oilskins. I half expected that he would fall apart like a pile of stones, rattling into a heap by the wheel. Instead he came alive.

First, he drew a breath. He raised his head and looked back; he turned it so slowly that I almost heard the creak of his neck bones. Then his right hand flew from the wheel and grabbed hold of my arm. The movement sent a ripple through his cape, and it was as though a great bird had swooped upon me.

I tried to pull away, but his bony hand was a clamp. He fixed me in his hollow stare and said, "Where did you come from?"

"Why, we came from the sea," said I. "In a boat, but it sank."

"How many?"

I held up my fingers to show him the count.

"Five?" He breathed rasping breaths and repeated the number. "That might be enough to hold them off."

"Who?" I asked.

With a wrench at my arm he pulled me to his side. "Take the wheel. Steer nor'east, boy; full and bye. That's Land's End where the surf's breaking ahead."

I could see the compass in the binnacle, the card tilting on a southerly heading. The sails sagged and flapped; the ship staggered to windward. Yet in the mind of the helmsman it was driving home to England with the canvas full of wind.

Boggis came no closer. "Where's the rest of the crew and the captain?"

"Dead and gone," said the helmsman. "It was murder, I call it."

The deck leaned heavily. The man's cape fluttered, and the bell—of its own accord—tolled sharp and clear.

"Murder and death," said the helmsman. "But no fear now; we'll hold them off. It's—"

He stopped in midsentence. A fly had landed on his

sleeve, and he was staring at it as though in fear. Another landed beside it, and a third settled on my wrist.

"You've let them loose!" he cried. "You fools. You bloody fools, you freed them."

They came by the dozen then, spotting the man's cloak with their black bodies, alighting on his hands, on his beard. He shook himself violently, flinging them off, and his fear turned to horror.

"They's only flies," said Boggis.

But the man turned and bolted for the rail. He crossed the deck in a clumsy shuffle, flailing his cape at the flies. He leapt to the rail, then swung back and looked at me.

"She's yours," he said. "All yours now, and the devil take you, for he will. You've let his demons loose."

The flies swarmed over him. They covered his scalp like a gleaming cap. They crawled on his beard, on his arms and his hands. There were so many flies that they made a cloud all around him. Then, with one backward step, he launched himself to the sea. I saw his wild hair streaming, his eyes all agog. There was no sound but the flutter of his cape.

I threw myself against the rail, and Boggis hurried to my side. But the man was gone; he'd vanished.

"Sank like a stone," said Boggis.

I didn't think so. To my mind's eye came a picture of the strange man swimming down toward the blackest depths, his feet kicking, his arms spread so that he sailed like a bird on the wings of his cape. He would dive so deeply, I thought, that there would be no chance he could ever come back.

The fin of the shark carved a circle in the sea and slid below the surface. It was the last I would ever see of that beast.

Within moments a bubble of red was welling up on the waves. The man's cape appeared again, now torn to tatters, and it fell away in our wake.

There was a groan and a tap, a creaking of wood. We saw the wheel turning, the ship swinging away from the wind. The sails flapped again as some filled and others collapsed. "The ship's going back to fetch that cove," said Boggis. But with a clang of the bell it steadied on the new course, wallowing through the swells.

It was heading nearly due south. I spun the wheel to bring its bow toward the north, but the ship only staggered like a stubborn old horse and plodded along to the south. I wasn't surprised. Even I knew there was more to steering a ship than turning the wheel. The sails would have to be set and braced and sheeted, and I doubted that five starving boys could do it.

"Where do you think she's off to?" said Boggis.

I shrugged. "Where the winds go, I suppose."

"But where's that?"

"Down to the south," said I. "To the ice and the storms."

"Lord save us." Boggis made the sign of the cross. "We've come from the fat to the fire, haven't we, Tom?"

# *Six*
## THE STORY OF A PHANTOM

We searched the fo'c'sle and the cabins in the stern, going everywhere in our little tangle of a group. It took all our courage to venture into the darkness, for we thought we'd find the hammocks and the sea berths full of corpses. But there was not a soul, living or dead.

In the fo'c'sle were the wooden chests of the sailors, the forks and bowls, the bits of handiwork half finished, now all in a ruin scattered across the floor. Only Weedle helped himself to the belongings of the vanished sailors. He put on a red stocking cap and a bright neckerchief. Round his waist he tied a crimson sash that hung to the deck. He must have fancied himself the image of a pirate, but in truth he lacked only a wooden sword to complete the picture of a boy in a dress-up game.

He strutted through the ship with that red sash flying as we searched every space. We found the same disarray in the cabins at the stern, though it was made of prettier and finer things. In what Midgely called the wardroom, a long table lay on its side, and six wooden chairs wrestled each other in the corner with their arms and legs interlocked. In the great cabin—the captain's quarters—everything imaginable could be seen on the floor. There was a string of pearls, the ruins of a harpsichord. There were small things, strange things, that must have been collected from every corner of the globe. There were clothes of silk, and polished shoes, and a beaver hat with a cricket bat driven through its top. But mostly there were books; there were books by the score.

There was something there to catch the fancy of each of us. We were boys, after all, and that cabin was like a secret cave, like the storehouse of a king. Even Midgely crawled through the heaps of debris, and cried out in great joy to find a wooden model of a sailing ship. Boggis unearthed a burst-open chest and its contents of figs and dates and chocolate. Weedle and Penny picked out the captain's jewelry, his rings and clasps, his watches with dangling fobs. As for me, it was the books I went after, and I rather lost myself as I sorted through the titles. With many came memories—some happy, as though of pleasant excursions I'd taken, others like terrible illnesses.

We were all gloating over our treasures when we heard the ghosts, or the spirits, or whatever it was that haunted that ship. There was a knocking like footfalls, and then a long groan of sadness. A rustling murmur, as though of breathing, came from the very hull.

We looked at each other, then scrambled as one for the deck. We dropped our little goods and fled from that space. I pulled Midgely along, stumbling over the piles of things in our way.

On the open deck was a cookhouse, and there we set up shop. If we sat too long in silence, and listened hard enough, we could still hear the hauntings from below. But the room was airy and bright, with a row of round windows in the wall, and we felt safer there than penned below with the ghosts. Boggis lit a fire in the cook's big stove, and soon the smell of boiling beef overpowered the stench of rot.

Of food, we had plenty. Of water, enough. There was a barrel by the hatch, half filled, though its contents were green and thick. In London I would have turned up my nose at the look of it, let alone the smell, but now I thought I'd tasted nothing finer.

Best of all, we had light. We had lanterns and lamps and candles, and on the first night we lit every one we could find, mindless of any pirates, and turned the ship into a great beacon of shimmering light.

Over the next few days we regained our strength as the ship carried us south. How it gladdened my heart to see the improvement in Midgely. I tried to confine him to bed; I told him he had the fever. But he admitted that he'd been drinking from the sea, and now claimed that the ship's green water was sweeter than honey. Certainly, it drowned the madness that had swollen inside him, and I was much relieved to see that my friend was not at death's door. As soon as I thought him well enough, I asked how we could steer the ship to England.

"Well, we can't," he said simply.

"Why not?"

"Because you can't steer a phantom, Tom. She's the *Flying Dutchman;* I told you that." We were sitting on the deck, leaning against the cookhouse wall. "Wind and weather means nothing to her. She goes where she likes."

He tipped back his head, as though he could see the masts and canvas. There was a breeze that carried the smoke from Gaskin's fire in swirls through the rigging. But the ship still wallowed along, rocking in the waves. The bell would have been tolling merrily if Gaskin hadn't lost his patience and torn away the clapper.

"You hear how the sails flap and slither?" asked Midgely. "There's wind to fill them, ain't there? She could put her railing down if she wanted. But she's plodding along instead, 'cause that's what she wants."

When it came to sails and ships, Midge could see more in his blindness than I with my sight. But to me the sails looked all higgledy-piggledy, and I wondered if Midge wasn't imagining what he *wanted* to see, or what he thought he *ought* to see if the ship was really his phantom.

"She found *us,* didn't she?" he said. "She came and picked us up, and now she's off for someone else. When the time's right, she'll hoist her skirts and run. That's the Dutchman's curse; he has to spend the rest of time dashing here and there, plucking souls from the sea."

"I don't know about the Dutchman," I said. "But the ship

is only a ship, and if we trim the sails we can go where we want."

"Don't even try," said he.

"But—"

"Don't even try."

That was the end of it, as far as Midge was concerned. Without him, I couldn't hope to get the ship turned around. So I got up and went into the cookhouse.

Benjamin Penny, and Weedle in his pirate clothes, were down on the floor playing a gambling game with dried beans. Boggis was bent over the stove, his chest heaving as he blew mightily into the fire. He liked fire, Boggis did. With the stove open, the flames leaping inside, he looked like a sort of fire god.

At his side was a book. He was holding a taper that he'd rolled from its pages, and smoke was wafting from its end, as though he held a magical wand.

From curiosity—nothing more—I picked up the book. It was handwritten, carelessly blotted, so that many of the words were lost in splashes and puddles of ink. More pages were missing than were left, but from the first passage I read, I could tell I was holding a strange story of the sea.

"We sail in search of Gold," it began. I had to chase flies from the page to see the letters. "But I fear all of Us will die before this Journey's done. Our Ship already is a tomb, though the Dead still hammer on the Coffin."

The next few words were drowned in ink, impossible to read. But I soon discovered that the ill-fated ship at the center of the tale was bound for the West Indies. It had last touched land at Java, where two sailors had joined the crew.

"A Fever came aboard with the new Hands," wrote the narrator. He had no respect for capital letters. "It was not Breakbone or Malaria nor any Illness of the Jungle. It was that Incurable Fever which comes from Gold! Within the hour the news had spread throughout the Ship, so that all knew of it from the boy to the Captain, and all shouted of it together. 'There has been a strike in Georgia! In the Wilderness of the New World! Nuggets of the Precious Metal lie on the ground like cinders on a path!' Ah, the Yellow Fever of the Gold. How it poisons the mind! At the mere sound of the Word there is no thought of anything but Gold—gold in nuggets, gold in veins, gold in fine dust. I was not immune from this myself. But none succumbed to the Fever as quickly and wholly as our Captain and the Mate."

The rest of the page was torn away, and the next few missing altogether. When the tale continued, the captain and half the crew had apparently perished. There were fewer than six left on the ship.

I was wondering about the story, and what might have happened, when I saw the smoking taper in Gaskin's hand.

Up I leapt and snatched it away. I waved it madly to extinguish the smoldering end, but it only burst into flame. I hurled it to the deck and stomped it to ashes.

Weedle and Penny and Gaskin were staring at me as though I'd lost my senses. They said not a word as I picked up the charred remains and unrolled the paper.

There was a list of names. It was headed "All Hands," and in a very different writing it named the members of the crew. At the top was "John Roberts, bosun's mate," at the bottom, "Henry Nore, the boy," with three of the names crossed over, and two others penciled in at the bottom. There were many strange marks and notations that I couldn't make out.

I asked Boggis, "Where did you get this?"

He pointed at the book.

"And where did you get *that*?" I said.

"I found it in the wood bin, Tom." He scratched his bottom. "I needed something for fire-starting."

There was no use being angry. I smoothed the burnt page and set it in among the others. I turned to the back of the book to see how the story ended.

"I feel my days are numbered. I can hold out no longer, and now only await my end. If I am lost, and this Account survives, let it be known that our Murdering Captain and the Mate were the undoing of every man, and the Ruin of our Voyage. May Justice be done! God rest us all!"

I knew the tricks of writers. They were crafty fellows who took bits of fancy and dressed them up to look like fact. But there was something about the ink-spotted journal, and the way it was written, that gave me no doubt it was a true account of the last days of the very ship we were on. I supposed that the writer had been the cook, and that his journal would have vanished forever if Boggis hadn't stumbled across it.

I carried the book outside and began, right then, to read it to Midgely. I told him only that it was a story of the sea, but he guessed very quickly that there was more to it than that. For a while he listened as I read.

> *"We were set South by the Winds. They blew with ferocity, forever foul. Not a man aboard had seen the likes of the Giant Seas that rolled on and on against*

*us. The ship was fairly swallowed between them. Our poor Cargo was thrown hither and yon, while the Men were tossed like dice in their beds. But the Captain paid no mind to the suffering. Under All Sail we made our westing. I feared we had fallen from the Grace of God."*

Midgely stopped me there. "Is this true or made up?" he asked.

I told him I didn't know. We were sitting with our shoulders touching, and he reached out and put his fingers on the paper, as though he could feel the ink and the scratchings of the writer's pen.

*"The strength of the Wind gave to the spray the power of Grapeshot. The men could not face into it, yet the Captain drove them to their work. On Christmas Day we saw God's face in the clouds, Bearded and angry. Every man saw it. Thomas Davis, the carpenter, fell to his knees at the sight. He raised his hands together and wailed for Forgiveness. For Mercy. The Captain himself took up the lash and gave the man such a flogging that it sickened the hearts of all Hands. Then he ordered the Men aloft, and piled canvas on canvas until it seemed the Ship would be driven under."*

There was a gap in the story where pages were missing. Then a boat was being launched, and men were being thrown into it as they struggled and screamed.

*"Their only crime was caring for the Ship. In the night they had eased a Topsail Brace, so that the Foremast would not be carried away. It was for that crime alone that our four poor Castaways were set adrift. The Captain and the Cruel Mate gave them guns and powder, a keg of water and Salt Horse each. But in those Monster Seas the Castaways had little hope of surviving. We had no doubt, as they fell away on the Stormy Sea, still waving and shouting for help, that we were seeing the last of them in this World."*

Midgely closed the book. With a flick of his hand he slammed it shut on my fingers. "It's made up," he said. "It ain't true."

"How do you know?" I asked.

"It's someone telling tales, that's what it is," said Midge. "It's true about the captain, and it's maybe true about the gold. But the castaways, that's rubbish. The Dutchman *picks up* the sailors, Tom; he don't cast them away."

"Well, then maybe we're not on his ship," I said.

"It says so right here!" Midge thumped the book with his fist. "The captain dared the storms, and God appeared and damned him for it. That's the story there, Tom. Like it or not, we're on the *Dutchman*. We'll spend the rest of our days plucking souls from the sea."

I laughed at his notions. But soon enough, I came to wonder if he wasn't right.

That night there were more stars in the sky than I had

ever seen. In their glow the horizon was crisp and flat. I could see a castle of ice floating miles away. The sea was so calm, the ship so steady, that I dreamed that night I was on solid ground.

Yet I soon woke to the eerie sound of wind in the rigging, half a moan and half a song. The ladles and pans that hung from the cookhouse walls were all at a slant, swaying as the ship plunged through the waves. There was a roar of water, and a motion that made me queasy.

Midgely was already awake. I said, "The sea's getting rough."

"No, it's the ship." There was a smile on his face. "She's sailing again."

He was right, as I learned when I stepped out of the cookhouse. Sails that had flapped from their stays now bulged with wind, pulling nicely. The ship leapt through the waves, flinging spray from the bow that pattered all over the deck. It was the sort of sailing my father had loved, and I could picture him grinning out across the sea with his clothes in a flap and his salt-covered beard in a tangle.

I imagined that a shift in the wind had sorted out the sails. But it certainly seemed that a ghostly crew had gone aloft to set and trim the canvas, missing only the main topsail. High above the deck, it was strangled and throttled by snarls of rope, flailing in the wind.

With the decks at a slant, the seas roaring by, we began to hear again the knockings in the ship. They followed each shuddering blast of a breaking wave, and came in chorus with the terrible moans from the timbers and planks. We could see the masts shaking, and hear the slosh of water rising in the bilge, but those moans sounded too human to come from mere wood.

Through the day we stormed along. But at nightfall the wind eased again, and the ship passed slowly through a field of ice. The southern sky lit up in glowing beams and arcs of light, so that the heavens seemed to cloak themselves in shimmering colors. The strange light played on the ice, and Midgely nearly cried because he couldn't see the shining castles and the slabs.

In the morning the field was behind us. There was only one bit of ice to be seen, and it lay straight ahead. A thick slab with a hummock in the middle, it was not very big, nor very tall, but it stood out plainly on the ocean. The hummock was stained a deep red, as though the ice still held the glow of heavenly lights.

Not until we were up close did I see that the ice was stained with blood, and that on its back rode a pair of ragged men.

## Seven

## THE CASTAWAYS COME ABOARD

My skin crawled at the sight of the men on their icy raft. A trick of wind and tide might have brought us together, but for a moment I believed that Midge was right, and that his *Flying Dutchman* was very real.

In that instant I didn't doubt that the ship would stop of its own accord, and the men would join us, and off we'd go to somewhere else. We gathered at the base of the big bowsprit, with no one at the wheel. Weedle's red sash whipped round his waist in the wind.

We saw white puffs rising from the ice, and thought the men were signaling with guns, though we never heard the cracking sound of the shots.

Each minute brought us thirty yards or so toward the ice.

Each minute made the scene before us more strange and terrible.

The two men stood at the low summit of their little island, not six feet above the sea. It seemed at first that they were dancing, for they reeled round and round at the top of the ice, their arms waving, their feet kicking. It seemed the fury of their dancing set their small world tilting to and fro beneath them. But it was really the ice that moved the men, and their dance was only a struggle to keep their balance. All around them the sea was white with froth, and great black fish kept bursting from the foam, battering at the ice.

I had to explain it for Midgely, who must have doubted my every word. "Fish don't come out of the water," he said.

Well, these ones did. They were long and fat, their black hides mottled by patches of white. From their backs rose enormous triangular fins, while their gaping mouths were full of teeth that a bear would have envied. Puffs of white spray shot up from the tops of their heads, scattering away on the wind.

Those black fish, like small whales but fierce as wolves, hurtled right from the water and crashed their bellies on the ice. Their tails churning the water, they drove themselves up onto the little island, until their own weight tipped them over, and they went rolling back to the sea.

The cold island, streaked with blood, rocked wildly in the attack of the black fish. At the summit the two men turned round and round to face each one. They had guns, but apparently no powder, for they were using their weapons like clubs, to bash at the heads of the creatures.

There was so much blood on the ice that the men must

have killed or injured one of the black fish. I imagined they'd been fighting for days, balanced at the top of their pitching island as the fish charged up again and again.

I called out as we shouldered our way toward them. The shadows of the sails raced ahead of us, over the foamy crests of the waves, over the ice and the black fish.

Like wolves at the coming of the shepherd, the creatures scattered and fled. At last the men looked up, and the sight of the ship suddenly looming above them must have been startling indeed. They cowered from it at first.

"We're going to run them down," I said. "How do we slow the ship?"

"She'll do it herself," said Midge. "You watch."

It didn't seem possible. Over the waves we charged like a great knight, the bowsprit our lance. The sea surged and foamed at the bow.

The ship didn't stop. But it did turn aside. The surge of waves breaking back from the ice caught the bow with a booming blow that nudged it away.

We all hurried to the waist in the hope that we might drag the men aboard. Gaskin swung out from the rail and stood on the ladder. We held his shirt and the waist of his pants, and he reached out with both arms just as the men dropped their guns and reached *up* for him.

The ship struck the ice and rolled it under. The men leapt up, clasping hands and arms with Boggis. The sudden shock of their weight nearly hauled every one of us over the side. But Gaskin held on, and the men twirled at the ends of his arms, skittering their feet on the tops of the waves like a pair of seabirds.

Walter Weedle leaned farther over the rail. One of the men looked up at him with the most surprised expression I'd ever seen. His eyes doubled in size, and his mouth gaped open. It seemed he truly believed he was seeing a pirate, that he had come to the ship of Blackbeard himself. But he must have glimpsed the boy within the clothes, for just as quickly the expression fell away.

So did the men, or very nearly. It took much puffing and cursing to bring them aboard, but at last we managed it. Side by side they stood on the deck, each dressed in many clothes, layer upon layer, all sodden with brine and blood. They gazed in wonder around the ship—down its length and up the masts—until their eyes settled on little Midgely.

"What happened to that one?" asked the taller of the two.

"He was blinded," I said.

"How?"

No one answered, though Benjamin Penny rather squirmed beside me. We were wary, like schoolboys sizing up a new teacher.

The taller man had tattoos on his hands, and a stare as cold as the ice that he'd come from. He was a frightening figure, but the other was twice as horrid and twice as scary. He looked like a pig, his ears so large and squashed, his head so round, speckled with lonely hairs. From his mouth came the most vile breath imaginable, for his teeth were brown and rotten.

"When I ask a question I expect an answer," said the taller man, turning to me. "What happened to that boy?"

His tone annoyed me. We had just saved his life, but he gave not a word of thanks, nor a how-do-you-do. I said only, "He's blind, not deaf. You can ask him yourself."

The piglike man drew a whistling breath through his teeth. Weedle's scar began to twitch. But the man with the tattooed hands only looked at me with the same burning gaze.

Weedle spoke quickly. "Sir, it happened long ago. In a prison hulk at Chatham, sir."

"At Chatham? You're convicts, are you?"

"Yes, sir." Weedle bobbed his head.

"Stowaways too?" Not a line or wrinkle had changed on the man's face. It was void of expression. "You escaped from Botany Bay, I suppose. Made your way aboard. Hid in the chain locker. Is that it?"

"No, sir!" cried Weedle. "We never even got to Australia, sir. We was lost and near to death—because of Tom Tin there—when this ship come along. It was days ago, sir."

"Where's the cook? Where's the carpenter?" said the man. "Where's everyone gone, boy?"

Weedle raised his shoulders in a huge, elaborate shrug. "We searched the ship, sir, and there weren't no one here—"

"The whole ship?"

"The whole bleeding ship, sir." Weedle drew a cross above his heart. "From top to bottom and end to end, and there weren't no one but the helmsman, who went off his nut and threw himself to the fishes. Tell him if that ain't true, Penny."

"I see." The man's tattoos were like rings on his fingers, bands of blue between his knuckles. When he stroked his beard, the painted rings seemed to tangle in his hairs. He studied Weedle for a while longer, then looked at each of our faces in turn, until he was staring into mine. "Your name's Tin, is it? Would you be the son of Redman?"

"Yes, sir," I said. "Do you know of him?"

"Who doesn't?" he asked. "I heard he was searching for you in the islands."

"Yes, he found me," said I. "But the cannibals took him."

There was no change in the fellow's expression, no sign at all of surprise at the news, not a hint of sadness nor pleasure. His hand kept running through his beard, stretching it down from his chin. "Did he mention a man called Beezley?"

"No, sir."

"We met only once." The man's hand fell from his beard. At last there came to his eyes a little gleam of light to show they were made of more than glass. It was a look of amusement, perhaps of satisfaction. "I'm Beezley," he said. "*Mister* Beezley. And this is Mr. Moyle. So if you're Redman's son, you can hand and steer, can you?"

*"Him?"* Weedle laughed loudly. "Tom's no sailor, sir. He was seasick at Chatham! He's afraid of the water."

"No matter," said Mr. Beezley, in his wooden way. "Mr. Moyle will teach him the ropes. He'll teach all of you, and you'll be wise to listen. When he says 'Jump,' you say, 'How high, sir.' And mind him well, if you're wise. Mr. Moyle eats children."

With this, Mr. Moyle opened his mouth and gnashed his brown teeth. It was a gruesome thing to see. But we weren't infants, not so easily frightened as that.

Round the feet of both men were puddles of reddish water. Their sodden clothes were dripping. Mr. Beezley loosened his coat. "Do as you're told and there'll be no trouble. That's all you need to know for now." He turned his back and walked away.

"Wait," I said. "Won't you tell me of my father, how you know him and—"

"No," he said flatly. "I've nothing to say to you, boy. We're not shipmates. And we're not chums. You'll do as you're told and ask no more questions."

"You've come to *our* ship, Mr. Beezley. Not the other way around." I spoke boldly, though in my innards I quivered. "I'd like to know where it is you've come *from,* Mr. Beezley."

"England," he said, and kept walking. The pair went straight to the water barrel. Mr. Moyle flicked the lid aside, and Mr. Beezley lifted the pannikin from its peg.

"You've sailed all the way from England on your iceberg?" I said.

Weedle snickered, then quickly clamped his mouth shut.

"Only a lubber would call that a berg," said Mr. Beezley. "It was barely a splinter." He dipped the pannikin into the water and stirred it about. Then he took a long drink before he spoke. "There was a sealing ship, boy. It was crushed in the ice down south. We took to the boats, but one by one they foundered. Mr. Moyle and myself would have drowned with the rest if we hadn't found that 'iceberg' of yours. There; now you know. And bear in mind that curiosity kills the cat."

He drank again, and again after that, taking in so much water that it gurgled inside him. Then he passed the pannikin to Mr. Moyle, who tried to pour his share straight down his throat, without shocking his rotted teeth. But still he twitched at the cold touch of the water. He twitched all over, from head to toe, as if a giant had shaken him like a dishcloth. He closed his eyes from the pain, and like that, with no sight, reached down and replaced the pannikin on its peg. It was as though he'd done it many times before.

Of course it came to my mind that these were the castaways set adrift from this very same ship. But if they were, why were they claiming to be sealers? What had happened to the others who had been cast away with them?

"How long were you adrift, Mr. Beezley?" I asked. "How many were in your company?"

"We didn't count the days, boy."

"Did you count each other?"

His glassy eyes suddenly glazed. There was such a look of anger that I had to turn away in a show of studying the sea.

"You're going to be trouble," he said. "I see that already. You like to think you're running the roost, don't you?"

Weedle spoke up. "That's true, sir; he does."

"It's as plain as the nose on his face," said Mr. Beezley. "But look where he's led you, boys. To a ship he can't steer, in a world where he's lost. He has no idea where he is, I wager."

Little Midge tried to answer, but was drowned out by Weedle and Penny. "No, sir, he don't!" they both said.

"Does he know where he's going?"

"No, sir!"

"A fine leader. Humbug!" Mr. Beezley slammed the lid on the barrel. "Well, my lads, what do you say we steer to the north?" His voice was rising. "What do you say I make sailors of you all?"

# I VENTURE ALOFT

Mr. Beezley extended his arms, and Weedle and Penny went to his side like monkeys to an organ grinder. Boggis didn't join them, and little Midge just turned away and wandered off. He sat by the mainmast, not quite facing us.

"You can steer where you like, Mr. Beezley," he said. "But it won't do you no good. This ship, she's a phantom."

I could see the gray crescents of his eyes, like old stones in his skull.

"She's the *Flying Dutchman*. That's why everyone's gone," he said. "The captain beat too long against the storms. The face of God appeared in the clouds on Christmas day, and the carpenter fell to his knees."

Beezley and Moyle might have frozen back into ice. They stood staring.

"What humbug!" said Mr. Beezley.

"It ain't humbug! The captain put four men in a boat and cast them away," said Midge. "They begged to be taken back, but he wouldn't listen."

"Who's been telling you this?" said Mr. Moyle. "You says you weren't on the ship, but—"

"It's in a book," cried Midgely. "Tom, he read it to me."

"Where's the book, Tom?" asked Mr. Beezley.

"In a box by the stove," I said.

Boggis had not yet lit a fire that morning, so there was no trace of smoke from the metal chimney. Yet Mr. Moyle shifted his gaze directly toward the cookhouse. Mr. Beezley said, "Go fetch it, boy."

I didn't like to be called boy, or to be sent on an errand by this thankless man. So I doddered along, looking up at the topsails, hoping that Mr. Beezley would shout at me to hurry. But he didn't.

I went into the cookhouse, pulled the book from the box, and shook out the list of all hands. Up and down I read that list before admitting there was neither a Beezley nor a Moyle among the names. But I was so certain that the men were our castaways that I kept the list—as if believing their names might somehow appear. I didn't mind giving up the book. Both Midge and I knew it by heart.

By the time I got back, the men had shifted to the side of the hatch. They had shed their heavy outer clothes, and now—in sailors' woolen shirts—looked like a pair of ragged

Robinson Crusoes. Mr. Moyle was on his knees, closing the iron dogs.

"Did you open the hatch, boy?" asked Mr. Beezley.

"We searched the ship," I said. "We told you that."

"What did you find down there?"

The question took me by surprise. If he knew the ship and everything about it, why would he ask?

"There was coconuts, sir," said Weedle, who stood dutifully at his side. "And breadfruit and flies. That was the lot, and it weren't worth the bother of looking."

"Then you shouldn't have looked," said Mr. Moyle.

I asked him why, but it was Mr. Beezley who answered. He stood straight and stiff as the deck tilted. "An open hatch can sink a ship," he said. "I would have thought any fool could see that."

He held out his hand for the book, snapping his fingers when I wasn't fast enough. Then he snatched it away and let the pages flutter apart. "Where's the rest?"

"We used it to start the fire," I said.

With a grunt he started reading at the middle of the book. I watched his eyes shift back and forth, his fingers flip the pages.

"Claptrap," he said. "Nothing but humbug." He closed the book. "It's the ramblings of a lunatic. Someone off his head with fever."

Midgely spoke up from his seat at the mast. "If you don't believe it, try turning the ship."

"Well, now that's what I mean to do," said Mr. Beezley. He looked up at the sails, squinting against the sun in the canvas. "We'll come about and go north. We'll make for warm waters. The Indies and Hispaniola and—"

"We'll make for England," I said. "That's where we want to go, Mr. Beezley."

"Is it?" He looked not at me, but to Weedle and the others. "You want to go back to the hulks; to the hangman perhaps?"

Weedle shook his head.

"Who would, but a fool?" Mr. Beezley held the book like a Bible, and spoke like a priest. "Follow me, my lads, and I'll make sailors of you all. Sailors and more, I promise you. We can all be rich beyond our dreams." His teeth showed in a white row through the tangle of his beard. "What do you say we go looking for gold?"

Just as the fellow had written in his book, the very word put a fever into Weedle and Penny and Boggis. They were like dogs who'd picked up a scent, their heads lifting, their whole bodies tensing.

Now, I had watched Mr. Beezley most closely, and I knew for a fact that he hadn't read the first pages of the book. I said, "Mr. Beezley, how do you know about the gold?"

"Doesn't all the world know by now?" he asked. "Only maroons on godforsaken islands haven't heard of the gold in Georgia."

This "took the wind from my sails," as my poor father would have said. Godforsaken islands were exactly where we had been, and we'd had not a shred of news in months.

Mr. Beezley walked to the rail and chucked the book out on the sea. It fluttered from his hand like a wounded bird. "Now, my lads, we've work to do," he said. "A ship to tend; a course to steer. We're sailing for gold!"

To this echo of the sailor's journal, Weedle and Penny gave three cheers, and we set about to turn the ship. Mr. Beezley took command, of course. He sent Benjamin Penny to the wheel, and Boggis to one of the many ropes at the side of the ship. He looked at Weedle's pirate clothes and said, "Go stand by the sheets there, Captain Kiddy." Even blind Midge was given a task. Mr. Beezley led him to a row of belaying pins, put his hands on a rope, and said, "When I give the word, you let that go. Understand?"

"It's the weather brace, is it?" said Midgely.

Mr. Beezley smiled for the first time. "Why, Mary's my mother!" he said in surprise. "That's just what it is. At least there's one of you with his wits about him."

Last of all he came to me. "You'll go aloft," he said.

I didn't have to obey, and I knew it. I could sit on the deck, refusing to work, but the ship would still be sailed where Mr. Beezley chose to sail it. He had taken it over, just as Mr. Mullock had taken over the longboat, as men would always do to boys. So I went to my chore, though not eagerly. I had been up in the rigging of a ship only once, and that time I had fallen from the maintop, straight into the sea. The thought of going again made jelly of my legs.

I looked up where Mr. Beezley pointed, at the high stick of the topsail yard, and let him think I understood his sailor's babble. "The brace is fouled with the Flemish horse," he said. "Mind it doesn't pitch you from the yard when you free it."

I began to climb the ratlines. I told myself that it was better to go north than do nothing, that there was much I could learn from Mr. Beezley. But I was only putting on a brave face, and that fell away as soon as I felt the roll of the ship, the sway and tremble of the ropes. My old fears got the better of me. I would have gone no higher if Mr. Moyle hadn't chased me. With a cry he came crawling up the rigging, nimble as a spider, shaking the ropes like a web. I looked down at him, and all I saw were his horrid teeth as he opened his mouth and shouted.

"Get up there, you trollop!" He came in a quick dart, hand over hand. "Get up or I'll bite you!"

It was no game he was playing. Mr. Moyle seemed furious, and I feared that if he caught me he would do just what he threatened, or worse. So up I went, and he chased me higher. I moved from fear, and from shame as well, for I heard the others laughing. Mr. Moyle chased me to the wooden top, through the lubber's hole and up again. Each time I looked down it was to see his piglike face a little closer. I scrambled up the topsail shrouds, and at last I reached the slender yard where the canvas hung.

I was then many feet above the sea, clinging to a teeter-totter mast. Sails flapped all around me, and the tangle of ropes writhed like so many snakes. Buntlines and braces and halyards and footropes were all wrapped around each other. I would have to shinny out along the yard to free them, and that stick of wood was swaying and plunging in the most alarming fashion.

Far below, the deck planks made a pattern of black seams and white wood. I saw Weedle's red sash, and the gray water coursing past the ship. Everything was moving three ways at once—up or down, back or forth, and side to side—and it all began to swim and blur as dizziness overtook me.

"Move yourself!" shouted Mr. Moyle, clawing his way up the rigging. He opened his mouth and gnashed his broken teeth.

In a flash I was out on the yard. I knelt astride it and inched my way along the wood. With the sail pressing at my legs, and the ropes pulling at my arms, it was all I could do to hold on. I stretched out along the end of the yard and pulled at the tangle of rope.

Without warning, it came loose. Something whipped at my shoulders, then all fell away with a great groan and a snap.

The yard twisted. The canvas opened with a shuddering crack. The whole ship leaned to the side, and with a small shout I tumbled from the yard.

# *nine*

## HOW I PLUCKED THE *DUTCHMAN*'S FLAG

It was Mr. Moyle who saved me. He was there as quick as a wink, one arm at my waist, a hand on my sleeve. He caught me in the moment that I fell, and swung me round so that my chest settled on the solid yard, and I stood in the bend of the footrope.

But there was nothing tender about him. As soon as his hand was free, he gave me a clout on the head. "Clumsy boy." He breathed his foul breaths into my face. "Hang on. She's coming about."

Then Mr. Beezley—his voice faint from the deck—called orders one after the other. The mast swung us high above the deck as the ship began to turn. Sails flopped across, and the yards shifted, creaking in their metal gear. The topsail shuddered and the whole mast shook, and I thought Mr. Moyle and I would be flung together out across the sea. But he held me tight—more tightly than I cared for—and the ship settled onto a new course. The sun came slanting through the sails now, making patches of gray and dazzling white, and the shadows of the ropes lay across them. Everything was moving, but slowly and grandly, like the soft rippling of albatross wings. My heart beat quickly, giving an extra shudder at the beauty of the wide sea all around, and the white curl thickening at the bow as the ship gathered speed.

"You saved my life," I said to Mr. Moyle. "Thank you."

He eyed me very strangely. "If you save a fellow's life, his life is yours. You know that, don't you? But no worry, lad." He smiled with the most gruesome leer. "I won't collect just yet, my boy. Collect I will, only not just yet."

He pinched my arm, but not from friendliness. With a push and a curse he sent me down again, and chased me all the way. I couldn't move fast enough for his liking, and twice he trod on my fingers as he followed me down the ratlines.

By the time I reached the deck, the ship was sailing nicely. We were reaching to the north with the yards braced back, the canvas taut and pulling. Mr. Beezley had given life to the wood and canvas, creating a creature that seemed full of joy to be charging along.

My companions, too, were in fine spirits. Old troubles forgotten, a new adventure ahead, they were ready to follow Mr. Beezley to the ends of the earth. "Where's the gold?"

they asked. "Does it lie all over the ground, Mr. Beezley?" Already their eyes were agleam, as though they'd been blinded by gold dust.

By nightfall our castaways had taken up quarters in the stern cabin, which had not been visited since our first morning aboard. From that moment on, as if the ghosts had left in fear, we heard nary a tap nor a breath as we pressed along.

In the rubble of abandoned things, the castaways found clothes that might have been tailored to fit. They shaved their beards, though Mr. Beezley left a strange strip along his jawbone, a hairy frame for a homely face. Mr. Moyle, clean-shaven, looked more than ever like a grunting swine.

Mr. Beezley lived up to his word, making sailors of us all. Under his guidance we overhauled the rigging from rail to truck, learning every term for every object in between. We took such a pride in handling that great ship, that every one of us—even I—was made better by it. Weedle proved himself handy with a marlinspike, and I often saw him sitting with Mr. Moyle, splicing rope in the sun. He was known by all as Captain Kiddy, which he took with good humor as he sported about in his piratical clothes. Benjamin Penny made a fine helmsman, though he had to stand on a wooden box to gain the height he needed. The giant Gaskin Boggis came to love going aloft. He would sit on the fore-topsail yard, high above the deck, drumming his heels against the wind-filled canvas.

Happiest of all was Midgely. With his *Flying Dutchman* so easily tamed, he had to give up the notion that we sailed a phantom ship. He thought it a fair trade, for Mr. Beezley made him the cook and, within the week, little Midge was at home with his chores. To watch him work was something of a wonder. He knew where every pot and pan was kept, and one would swear he had the eyes of a cat as he went bustling about, turning our maggot-ridden supplies into hearty meals. It gave him hope, and a belief that his life hadn't been ruined with the loss of his eyes. "That might be the best thing what ever happened to me, Tom," he told me once. "There weren't no one what was going to take no urchin out to sea. But now it's a different kettle of fish, ain't it, Tom? Now I'm an urchin what can cook."

Even I, at times, enjoyed those days, and especially my turns at the wheel. They began before dawn and ended in daylight, so that I marked the rising of every sun. I found an enormous beauty in the ship's windborne passage, a great comfort to be going north at such a steady rate. I began to imagine that I was really on my way home after all. From Georgia, I thought, I might easily find a ship to take Midge and me to England, if I could beg the fare from our castaways. That didn't seem like much to ask, though there was a lurking dread in my mind that it would never happen, that some terrible fate had come aboard with our strange sailors. Certainly, it was hard to believe I was "doing the handsome thing" as long as I left myself in the hands of Mr. Beezley.

And so the miles went rolling past, and I spent much time alone. Often I thought of my mother and my father; sometimes I could bear to think of them no more. Then I studied the ship, learning how it worked, and *why* it worked. It was no puzzle how the wind could push it along from behind, but a great mystery how another wind could *pull* it from ahead. I never tired of gazing at the sails, trying to learn the secret.

With every change in the weather, my seasickness bubbled up. Or more. But my *fear* of the sea all but disappeared. I never again had to be driven aloft, and one stormy day I found myself balanced on the topgallant yard without a thought of falling or fainting. The horizon was pitching and slanting, the yard tossing like a horse, but the only thought in my head was of tying a proper reef knot.

That moment I made it my ambition to climb even higher, to reach the very top of the mainmast. I went at it in spurts, scrambling up through the shrouds until I dared go no higher. It took me days to reach the top, but at last I did it. I stood on slender ropes, with the great gulf of sea and sky below me, and—trembling like an insect—I touched my palm to the very tip of the mast.

To prove that I had been there I tore away the shreds of the old flag. The wind had tangled them into one long braid, and the sun had bleached the braid to white. I held it in my teeth as I descended to the deck. With much delight I set it out for Midgely on the counter of the cookhouse.

He smiled when he touched it. He unrolled the braid with his small fingers, working the tangles from threads and shards of cloth.

"Wouldn't it be funny if this was really the flag of the *Flying Dutchman*?" he said. "People would ask, 'Where did you get that old flag?' and we would say, 'Oh, only from the *Flying Dutchman,* that's all.' Wouldn't it be grand?"

I wasn't really listening. I was too intent on the pattern

that was appearing under Midgely's fingers. I saw green and purple, and fragments of gold. Much more cloth had been blown away in the wind than remained for me to see, but I pieced it back together in my mind. The last time I had seen such a flag was on the ship that carried us from England toward Australia. It was the pennant flown by all of Mr. Goodfellow's ships.

What a turn that gave me. I had escaped from one of his ships only to get aboard another. It was as though Mr. Goodfellow had hounded me nearly to the shores of the frozen continent. I thought I could never be rid of him.

I tore the flag from Midgely's hands. I squashed the cloth in my fist, set it aflame in the stove, and watched it burn. I didn't imagine that my discovery was really the first of three incidents that would, again, put a twist into the river of my life.

The next came only a day later. It was my turn at the wheel, and dawn was breaking. As they did every morning, Beezley and Moyle came up from below with the rising of the sun. Mr. Beezley, as always, took a moment to stand at my side and study the compass.

He was turning away to join Mr. Moyle at the stern when a strange sound came over the sea. It was a cry of loneliness, a plaintive mewling in the vanishing darkness.

"What the devil's that?" said Mr. Beezley, stopping in his tracks.

"Do you think it might be mermaids?" asked Mr. Moyle, with all seriousness.

"Humbug!"

The cry came again. Mr. Moyle and Mr. Beezley hurried to the side of the ship.

"If it's not mermaids, then what is it?" said Mr. Moyle.

Ahead of the ship a bit of ice appeared. It was the first we had seen in many days, and the last we would see on the voyage. It had been carried very far, and was nearly fully melted.

The sounds changed to frantic barks and yelps.

"It's *dogs,*" said a wondering Mr. Beezley. "How on earth could dogs be there?"

We passed within fifty yards of the ice. It seemed to turn to solid gold as it took on the light of the rising sun. Spotted across it were small gray shapes that looked very doglike indeed, until they reared up from the ice. If these were dogs they were legless; but of course they were only seals.

Perhaps my eyes were better than those of the castaways, but I would have thought that a pair of sealers might have known their quarry more easily. The two peered over the rail for the longest time before Mr. Beezley laughed. "Why, they're seals," he said.

"Fancy that," said Mr. Moyle.

The third incident followed within the week. As the nights grew warm, and then hot, a richer stench began to rise from the closed-over hatches. Again we heard the buzzing of flies.

By chance, Midgely uncovered another page from the journal—or a fragment of a page. It was rolled into a taper, charred at the end from Gaskin's fire-lighting. It had been burnt and water-dipped, so that only two paragraphs could be read. From those, one sentence leapt out at me.

"He cares nothing for what lies below the breadfruit."

Little Midge and I sat and wondered. All that evening we did nothing but ponder. What could lie below the breadfruit?

In the dark of the midnight watch, while Beezley and Moyle and Penny were sleeping—while Weedle had the wheel—I took a lantern and went off to find out. Midgely and Boggis helped open the dogs on the hatch. Then Boggis lifted the heavy lid, and I slipped under its edge, down through a horde of flies.

# *ten*

# I LOOK BELOW THE BREADFRUIT

The flies were so thick that I breathed them in. I felt them on my teeth, in my nose, in the back of my throat. So I took off my shirt and tied it like a mask round my mouth. And with my lantern held high, I went down.

The fruit squelched under my bare feet, bubbling pulp between my toes. It reminded me of the first day of my adventure, when I had become glued in the foul mud of the river Thames. Now, as then, I feared that I would sink so deeply I could never get out.

But I came to a sudden and solid stop only knee-deep in the breadfruit and coconut shells. I kicked a clearing round my legs and found a set of iron hinges. In a few minutes more I uncovered a heavy clasp and a handle, and the edges of a trapdoor. I scooped away the coconuts, kicked aside the breadfruit, then knelt down and lifted the handle.

A cascade of swollen breadfruit went plopping through the trapdoor, into the darkness below me. The flies swarmed up—or down; I couldn't tell. They merely blackened the lantern in their thousands. They turned the air to muddy water that swirled in eddies and ripples. I crouched at the edge of the hole, waiting for the blackness to settle.

Soon I saw bodies down there. Or parts of bodies. In the rolling gait of the ship, my lantern's light slid through the shadows and the swarms of flies. I saw faces and hands, arms and ribs. I saw row upon row of dark-skinned people, all chained to the deck, and all deathly still.

I understood everything in that one, terrible look. The real cargo of the ship, its true business, had been hidden below a false panel. What we'd thought were the sounds of a haunted ship had been the last breaths of these people. The taps on the planks had been signals for help. The groans when the ship had pitched hard—those frightening groans that had raised our hairs—had been the sounds of unbearable suffering.

All because of Mr. Goodfellow!

I now knew why he had so much trouble finding captains for his ships, and why he'd sent my father on a winding route through the cannibal islands instead of straight to England from Australia. Slavery was the "new venture" that had sent him out to seek my father.

The flies were settling now on the bodies below, and they gave a shimmering life to the limbs and faces and torsos. Skinned with flies, the people seemed to twitch and turn in their chains.

I counted three or four children among the adults. They all lay on their sides, each facing the back of another, as one would arrange bananas in a row. All together there must have been three score, and I thought that all had perished. But I heard a rattle of chains, that chinking of iron that I would never forget in all my life, so often had I heard it on the wretched hulk *Lachesis*.

I drew closer to the edge of the hole, sending more breadfruit tumbling down. A shift in the lantern's light showed me a man unlike the others.

Among the naked bodies, he alone was fair of skin, and he alone was dressed from head to toe. He wore a stocking cap and a crimson sash.

At first glance he looked like Walter Weedle. I remembered how Mr. Beezley had stared in shock at his first sight of the red-clad Weedle, and I knew he had mistaken him for this man in the hold.

I shook my lantern, listening for the slosh of oil inside. Finding plenty, I set it down at the edge of the door and clambered through the hole. The light chased the shadows from the man with the sash, and the flies went swirling again.

The fellow was barely alive, as I soon discovered. It seemed to take all his strength just to open his eyes and turn his head toward me. He said one word: "Water."

I had brought none with me. But it was a simple task to squeeze the liquid from a spongy breadfruit, and wet his lips with that. He took it eagerly, even greedily, licking every drop. He sucked the breadfruit like a great teat, until the juices poured over his face and dribbled on the deck, then turned his head and slurped them from the plank.

He had to catch his breath after that, wheezing in the foul air. "Thank you," he murmured. "God bless you."

I told him my name and he blessed me again. He moved in his irons, jingling the metal as he reached for my hand. His fingers were cold as death.

"The captain," he said. "Where is he?"

"Gone," I told him. "They're *all* gone, from the captain to the boy."

His eyes closed, and such a peaceful look came over him that I thought he had passed away. But he wasn't done yet with his dying. "A dream, then," he murmured. "I dreamed he was here. I heard his voice."

I gave him another drink. He managed to lift his head slightly, then eased back with a sigh.

"Where were you captured?" I asked.

He shook his head, as though he didn't understand.

"You were taken as a slave," I said. "Where was—"

"No!" said he. "Never a slave." He tugged at his irons as he pulled me closer. "I was part of the crew, Tom. I was the cook."

"The *cook*?" I asked. "You kept the journal?"

He nodded, just enough to set a tingle through his chains. "You found my story? Remember it, Tom, and tell them in England. Tell them everything."

"I will," I promised.

He settled back. Clearly, he had only moments to live. I found another breadfruit and let him drink its juice. "Did you know a man called Beezley?" I asked.

"Beezley!" His eyes opened wide. His voice became harsh. "Beastly, you mean! Of course, I knew Beastly."

Those were his last words. His breath gargled, and his

head fell back on the deck. With his hand in mine, his eyes like saucers, he had gone to his maker.

I couldn't escape him fast enough. I nearly *leapt* through the hatch. I lowered the door over the sight of those slaves and those flies, covered it quickly, and snatched up the lantern. All in a state, I flung myself out to the open air.

Midgely and Boggis were waiting. Midge had his bucket, brimming with water that he'd drawn from the sea. The tail of its rope was still in his hand. "Have a wash, Tom," he said. "Then tell us what you seen."

Boggis went round the hatch, closing the dogs as I scrubbed my arms and legs. We moved up to the foredeck, where we seated ourselves around the capstan like petals on a flower.

"So we heard them dying?" said Midge, when I'd told my tale. "Oooh, it gives you the shivers, don't it?"

"We could have saved them," I said.

"Not if we didn't know they was there," said Boggis.

I watched the stars slide through the rigging, swinging in and out from behind the sails. "One thing's certain," I said. "The cook knew Mr. Beezley."

"How could he?" said Boggis.

"Because your wonderful Mr. Beezley was on this ship," I said.

"Maybe not," said Midge. "Did the cook say *when* he knowed him?"

"No," I said. "I suppose he didn't. But when Mr. Beezley saw Weedle in his red sash he—"

"He thought he saw a lunatic," said Boggis.

The pair had an answer for everything, and I didn't want to argue. I decided that I would have to challenge Mr. Beezley straight out, and that I would do it as soon as he came up to the deck in the morning. During my watch at the wheel I rehearsed the things I would say. When the sails began to take their gray shapes in the blackness, I put a strop on the spokes to stop the wheel from turning and went to stand by the hood of the companionway, where the castaways would soon emerge.

I quickly regretted it. The pair came tramping up the ladder, unaware that I was waiting. Mr. Beezley was talking.

"I put the word in Weedle's ear," he said.

"Eager as eggs, is he?" asked Mr. Moyle, hidden below me.

Mr. Beezley laughed. I heard him take another step toward the deck. "The cripple won't be any trouble. Nor will blind Batty. I don't know about the big bruiser."

"He's stupid, but he's strong," replied Mr. Moyle. "I want to see the look on King George's old mug when he gets a squint of Gaskin Boggis."

What a riddle that became! It was scarcely possible that someone like Mr. Moyle could expect an audience with King George IV, and even more unlikely that he would take Boggis along. Yet entwined in the riddle was a small thread of hope. If Mr. Moyle even *imagined* that he might meet with the King of England, where could he be heading but to England itself?

"Now what of Tom Tin?" asked Mr. Beezley. "That boy's a nuisance. I want him out of the picture."

"Soon," said Mr. Moyle.

"One fell swoop is best, don't you think?"

The pair was nearly at the deck. I saw one of Mr. Beezley's tattooed hands reaching for a hold to hoist himself up. In a moment he would emerge and find the wheel deserted.

# *eleven*

## MIDGELY REMEMBERS A TALE

The top of Mr. Beezley's head appeared. I could hear Mr. Moyle pressing up behind him, and my heart was in my throat.

It was only sheer luck that saved me.

The ship stumbled on a wave. Held by the strop, like a dog on a leash, it couldn't round up to the wind. Instead it rolled sideways, sending spouts of green water shooting through the scuppers. Mr. Moyle, caught out of balance, stumbled backward down the stairs. He must have clutched on to Mr. Beezley, for a string of thumps and oaths came through the hatch, then a howl of pain from Mr. Moyle.

I dashed to the wheel and lifted the strop. The spokes cracked my knuckles as the ship reeled upright. The water that had surged across the deck went surging out again, tumbling over the rail in froth and cream.

When Mr. Moyle came up to the deck he was holding a hand to his jaw. Either he had thumped it on something, or Mr. Beezley had thumped it for him. The pain from those rotted teeth must have been terrible, for his eyes were watering. "You half-boiled nizzie!" he growled. "I'm going to—"

"Mr. Moyle!"

Both of us turned to look at Mr. Beezley. The way that Mr. Moyle fell instantly silent and shuffled off to the rail made me see that he, too, was being kept on a leash of sorts. I was afraid of what could happen if he was ever turned loose.

The beard that framed Mr. Beezley's face was growing ragged. It reminded me then of a lion's mane, and it shook as he walked to my side. He looked down at the compass.

"I know what you're thinking, boy," he said. "I know what goes on up here." He tapped my head—hard—with his knuckles. "You'd like to see the end of me, wouldn't you?"

"Why should I want that?" I asked.

"Because you fear me," said he, very matter-of-fact. "And well you should, boy. Yes, well you should."

Mr. Beezley was never more frightening than when he talked of dark things. I couldn't bring myself to ask about the cook, to challenge him at all, and only stood there with shivers in my neck.

I was glad when he wandered away, until I heard him muttering behind my back with Mr. Moyle. It seemed his "one fell swoop" might happen right then. But I realized that as long as we kept at sea we were safe, as there were barely enough people to work the ship as it was.

North we went, another hundred sea miles from dawn to dawn. Then, again, I was standing at the wheel, waiting for the castaways to come up from below. But today they were late, and they still hadn't appeared when Benjamin Penny came to take my place.

He climbed the ladder and made straight for the mizzen shrouds, where he kept his wooden box. He untied the lashings and dragged it over.

"Where's Mr. B?" he said. "Where's Mr. Moyle?"

"Still below," I told him.

"Well, push off," he said. "Your turn's done."

Penny loved to steer the ship. It was probably the first time in his life that he'd been given a useful task, and—like Weedle—he worshiped Mr. Beezley for this trust he'd been given.

"Go on. Hop it, Tom." He pushed the box against my feet and climbed aboard it, trying to crowd me from the wheel. His webbed hands prodded at my arms; his twisted bones knocked on my hip.

I couldn't bear the touch of Benjamin Penny. I gave up the wheel and let him squirm into place behind it. He glanced up at the sails, his sharp little teeth giving him the wicked smile of a cat.

"You've pinched her," he said. "Look at them luffs."

By instinct I did as he said, surprising myself that the language of sailing men had become such a part of me. I saw the sails rippling along their windward edges and knew he was right; I had let the ship wander too close to the wind.

It gave Penny a great pleasure to point this out, and he made it clear that he had to correct the mistake I'd made. He heaved mightily on the wheel, though a touch would have been enough.

"Don't bother waiting for Mr. B," said Penny. "He'll be glad he don't have to see your face. He don't care figs for you, Tom."

"Nor for you," said I.

"Humbug!" So Penny had even adopted his hero's words. "He's taking me and Weedle to look for gold. But he ain't taking *you,* and he ain't taking Batty neither."

*Batty*. It was the second time in as many mornings I'd heard that name.

"You wait," he said. "Mr. B's got something planned for you. Poz! He does."

"What sort of thing?" I asked.

He shrugged, gloating horribly. "All I know is, I wouldn't want to be in *your* shoes."

"Perhaps you are," I told him. "What if he's planning the same thing for you?"

A look of doubt came and went on Penny's face. "Humbug!" he said again. "Mr. B's taking me under his wing, he is, and if you say otherwise I'll stick you for it, Tom. I swear to God I'll stick you."

I went to the cookhouse and watched Midgely bustle about, filling a bucket with potatoes. With the ship sailing, and the whole room at a slant, everything seemed to hang at a weird angle. Skillets and towels swayed far from the wall, while the bucket seemed to float up from Midgely's hand. It was a sight that still turned my stomach, and I kept looking out at the horizon.

"What do you know about the gold in America?" I asked.

"Only that we're going looking for it," said Midge. "Funny, ain't it? I can't see it, and you don't need it, but there we go."

"Did you know Gaskin's going to meet King George?" I asked next.

Midge laughed out loud. "Oh, he ain't going to meet no King. Who told you that?"

"Mr. Moyle. I heard him tell Mr. Beezley he's taking Gaskin to meet the King."

"You didn't hear him right, Tom." Midge put his bucket on the table and climbed up on a chair. "How's Mr. Moyle going to meet King George if he's digging for gold in America?"

I watched him peel potatoes, his knife going back and forth. The parings piled up on the table, but he was mindless of the brown bits of rot that he was uncovering.

"And why would the King want to meet either of *them*?" he said. "No, Tom, it doesn't make sense. You didn't understand."

Well, I did understand. I knew that we would arrive in the West Indies, or America, and that Boggis would meet the King. It sounded most unlikely, but somehow it *had* to make sense.

As we traveled on, I saw the North Star rising higher each night. Over the courses and over the topsails it went, sailing by in the darkness. The great plow was like the hand of a huge clock, its turning a reminder that our journey would end.

I was sitting on the hatch, gazing up at it one night, when Midgely groped out of the darkness and appeared at my side. His cold hand touched my arm.

"Tom, I woke up remembering," he said. Penny and Boggis were asleep in the cookhouse, and Weedle was steering. "Those sailors what talked to me mam? There was one what knew a fellow so mean they called him *Beastly*."

I thought of the man in the hold, his last words uttered in fear. *"Beastly, you mean. Of course, I knew Beastly."*

"You see, Tom, it's like Beezley, but it ain't," said Midge. "But he was a captain, Tom, this fellow. They called him Captain Beastly."

"Oh, Midge, of course!" I cursed myself for being too stupid to see it sooner. "That's why he's not on the list, why he's not in the story. Mr. Beezley was never cast away by the captain. He *was* the captain."

"You see, that's what I wondered," said Midge. "But why would the captain leave his ship? How would the captain get marooned on a bit of ice?"

Well, I had no answers for that. "What else did the sailor tell you?" I asked.

"Only that Captain Beastly flogged three men to death 'cause someone pinched his salt," said Midge. "Only that he had a price on his head, that's all."

I could see the picture coming together. My father had always told me that Goodfellow ships were commanded by thieves and cutthroats. I already knew beyond doubt that our Mr. Beezley had been on this ship, and now I thought I knew why he would always deny it. He was heading for the goldfields so that he might vanish into the wilds of America.

But what about King George? That remained an absolute mystery as we bashed our way north through the trade winds. The following week we made our landfall.

A chain of scattered islands appeared on the horizon. We worked our way between them, into the wondrous world of the Caribbean, and soon arrived at Mr. Beezley's destination.

It was a large island—a beautiful place—with a sheltered bay on its southern side. A British flag was flying at the end of a long pier, and the wind smelled richly of earth and trees. As we beat our way toward the pier, five people emerged from the shore, walking out along it.

Mr. Beezley had the wheel. We had already hauled up the courses and the gallants, and now we lowered the jib, leaving only the main topsail. With his mane rippling from his cheeks, his tattooed hands on the spokes, Mr. Beezley aimed the bowsprit right for the pier. He went on so steadily that the people scattered from our path, and even Mr. Moyle looked worried. But at the last moment he rounded the ship into the wind and brought us neatly alongside. After thousands of miles, and days too many to count, we came to a stop at last.

Mr. Beezley looked out onto the pier. There were two men and three boys, brown-skinned all but one. "Why, there he is!" Up went his hand, and he waved gaily. "Good day to you, King George."

*twelve*

# THE KING STRIKES A BARGAIN

The pale-skinned man stepped forward. He was a stout little fellow in old-fashioned breeches, like a stuffed chicken strutting down the dock on a pair of fat drumsticks. He was wearing a hat of woven grass, and a belt into which he'd jammed a huge pistol. He motioned to his native companions, who set about to secure the ship.

"Your Majesty!" Mr. Beezley shouted. "Please, come aboard."

The little fellow put a hand on his pistol and clambered over the rail. From a string around his neck hung a set of keys so bulky that it nearly toppled him forward.

Now, there was nothing kingly about the man. Sweaty and pink, he was the most ordinary sort of fellow. He could have been a costermonger without a barrow, or a crossing sweeper who'd forgotten his broom. But poor blind Midgely, at my side, knelt on the deck. He touched one knee to the wood and bowed his head. "Your Majesty," he muttered.

"It's not the *King,*" I snapped. "It's only a funny man in a funny hat. Now get up, Midge."

The fellow scowled at Mr. Beezley. He raised his little hat and wiped the sweat from his forehead. "You're more than a month behind times," he said. "We gave you up as lost."

"There was trouble, George," said Mr. Beezley.

"Open the hatch. We'll have a look below."

"There's no need—"

"Indulge us!" shouted the fellow in a voice that was twice his size. "We would like to see what you've brought."

Weedle was hovering nearby like a servant. He hopped forward now. "I'll do it, Mr. B."

"Shut up, you toad-licker!" roared Mr. Beezley. "Go and stand by the starboard rail. All of you stand over there."

We did as he told us. Weedle skulked with his tail between his legs, and Benjamin Penny glanced about like a rat emerging from darkness. I saw Midgely feeling the air with one hand, and regretted my sharp words. I led him to the rail and kept him at my side.

Mr. Beezley and Mr. Moyle circled the hatch, freeing its metal dogs. The little King only watched as they heaved the lid aside. A cloud of flies welled up, and a waft of that terrible stench. Mr. Moyle stepped over the high coaming, into the breadfruit and coconuts. He cleared the trap and hauled it open.

The King peered down into the hold. "Good Lord!" he said. "Good Lord almighty." He turned away, clearly sickened by what he'd seen. "We deal with slaves, not corpses," he said.

Neither Weedle nor Penny had any understanding of our true cargo. One turned to the other, and together they asked, "What's down there?"

The King was already retreating from the ship. Mr. Beezley followed him over the rail, crying, "Wait, Your Majesty! Don't get all high and mighty; there's more than what you see."

"What else could there be?" said the King.

Beezley and Moyle and the little man stood together on the pier. They talked quickly and quietly, with much pointing and head-shaking. Mr. Beezley, especially, kept glancing toward us.

"Mr. B's striking his bargain with that little cove," said Weedle. "When he's done it's on to the goldfields for us. But not for Tom Tin."

I had come to the same conclusion. With our voyage over, and the ship secured, there was no need for me anymore. Mr. Beezley wouldn't wait much longer to get me "out of the picture."

The cloud of flies brought a cloud of birds. In flashes of yellow and ochre and brown, they darted through the rigging, over the cookhouse, up and down the deck. Their twitters and shrieks were beautiful to hear, but unnerving as well. I had become too used to the sounds of the sea, the rush and pulse of waves that still echoed in my ears.

On the dock, King George took off his hat to flap it at the birds.

Mr. Beezley's voice was growing louder. "Keep your money, you old pirate," he said. "It's shovels and picks and powder I want."

"All right, all right," said the King. "Bring your lot ashore."

As the King started down the dock, Mr. Beezley reached out and snatched the pistol from his belt. The little man tried to catch it as it soared up past his head, and looked for a moment like a fat boy trying to catch a runaway balloon. Then he made sure that his keys still hung at his neck, and, with his hand on his shirt, he hurried away.

"No less than three barrels of powder!" shouted Mr. Beezley. "And have your men clean up the ship. It's disgusting down below."

The King trotted down the dock with the birds swooping round his head. Mr. Beezley, now armed, came over the rail again. He bounced the gun in his hand, turning it end for end, then tightened his grip and cocked the hammer. Behind him came Mr. Moyle, who rubbed his flattened nose and smiled a piggy smile.

"Off the ship!" said Mr. Beezley. He pointed the gun at my face. "Go on. And take the blind boy with you. You've come to the end of your road, Tom Tin."

I took Midgely's hand. He looked sad and disappointed as I led him toward the rail.

"Hurry!" shouted Mr. Beezley. "The rest of you behind him."

"Except for me, right, Mr. B?" said Weedle. "Ain't that—"

"All of you!"

I kept hold of Midgely's hand. I led him onto the pier, where the British flag curled above us in the breeze. Weedle and Penny and Boggis came after us, and the fellows who'd tied the ship now went aboard, plodding glumly to their dreadful task of cleaning the hold.

"Keep walking," said Mr. Beezley.

The pier was made of planks set crosswise, so that the water flickered in the narrow gaps between them. My eyes knew it was solid and still, but my legs didn't, nor did my brain. Those planks seemed to heave and bend, and I staggered toward the land. One moment I bumped against Midgely, the next we fell apart to the lengths of our arms.

As we came closer to the shore, I saw a clearing in the trees. More of it came into view with every step we took. There was a woman hanging laundry on a line, struggling with sheets that were white and blowzy. A little girl with a bright pinafore and golden curls was playing nearby at a lonely game. With the sun in the trees, and the birds flitting past, we might have come to a place as pleasant as Fiddler's Green.

I could hear Boggis walking heavily behind us, Weedle and Penny whispering together. Midge tugged my hand as we tramped along. "Where are we, Tom?" he said. "It feels gloomy, like it's raining but it ain't. Tell me the truth now. What do you see?"

"A mother and her child," I said. The gold-haired girl was seated at a tiny table, and in other chairs sat her dolls, propped upright like bits of lumber. "She's having a tea party," I said.

"What else?" asked Midge. "Tom, I can hear irons."

There was a wooden fence appearing now, two fathoms tall or more. It reminded me of Mr. Moyle's brown teeth, for the poles were of a ragged height, chiseled into pointed tops.

We were walking toward it, driven on by Mr. Beezley. I could hear him clicking the hammer on his gun, and the others muttering as they trudged behind me. On shore a gate swung open in the wall. The little King stepped through, looking smaller than ever in the oversized door, like one of the girl's little tea-party dolls.

"That's far enough," said Mr. Beezley, and we all came to a halt.

Midgely crouched on the dock. He rubbed his hands along one of the planks, then over the one beside it. He was feeling the edges of a shallow rut that was worn into every plank, that stretched the length of the dock from the shore to its end. "Tom, please tell me the truth," he said.

I knew right away what had made that rut. I had helped to grind similar marks into the decks of the prison hulk *Lachesis,* where the chains on our ankles had dragged behind us.

Midgely knew it too. "Holy jumping mother of Moses," he said. "We're going to be sold as slaves."

# *thirteen*

## I REACH THE END OF MY ROAD

On the heels of the King came six large men. They walked Indian file, in a rattle of metal, for they were burdened down with loads of chain and shackles, with shovels and picks and axes.

Round the neck of each man was an iron collar, and to each collar was fixed the end of a heavy bar. The six men, coupled into a human train, had to keep the same pace with their bare feet pounding. They rocked to the left together, then rocked to the right as one, and with each step came the jingle and rattle of metal.

The little girl looked up from her tea party to watch the slaves go by. There was a small silver pot in her hand, tipped above the tiny cups. A bit of hair had fallen across her face, but she didn't brush it aside. She watched the slaves with no expression, as lifeless as her dolls.

Across the lawn, her mother dropped the laundry basket. She ran to the table, swooped on the girl, and snatched her off to the house. The girl cried, reaching back, because one of her dolls had toppled.

Mr. Beezley went past us and down the dock toward the little King. I grabbed Midge and whirled him around, thinking we'd run back to the ship. But Mr. Moyle was there to stop me.

"You'll not be going anywhere, boy," said he.

The dock was not more than eight feet wide, and about the same height above the water. There was nowhere to go except into the sea, and I couldn't do that. I imagined plunging to the bottom, where yellow sand rippled faintly in the sunlight. The vision of my sister pulled drowned from the Thames came suddenly to my mind, followed by a memory of my cold tumble from the prison hulk. I remembered my sense of panic in the water, and knew I couldn't leap from the pier even to save little Midgely.

The slaves came tramping with their chains. The heaviness of their steps sent trembles through the pier.

Ten paces away, they set down their loads. They made a heap of the chains and irons and tools, then turned back for more. There wasn't room to turn the human chain on the pier, so each man pivoted within his collar, trying to hold the iron apart so that it wouldn't scrape away his skin.

The King put his foot on the stack of shovels. "Imagine three barrels of powder added to this. Do you know, I believe it's a generous offer."

"Not enough," said Mr. Beezley. "Not after the troubles I've weathered to get here. A mutinous crew; a fever that felled them like flies. We had to abandon ship—Mr. Moyle and myself—in a sieve of a boat that sank within days. We survived on a bit of ice as big as your tabletop."

So *that* was the tale of Captain Beastly. He had abandoned his own ship in fear of the fever and a crew who despised him. Mr. Beezley—and his "Cruel Mate," Mr. Moyle—were castaways sure enough. But they'd been cast away by themselves.

Mr. Beezley kept ranting away, listing his troubles. "I've been attacked by blackfish," he said, "and blackened by frostbite. I've been made a nanny to sniveling boys, and—"

"All right, all right! But this is highway robbery!" The little King quivered in anger. "What's Mr. Goodfellow going to say when he hears about it?"

"He never will," said Mr. Beezley. "The ship will rot away in New Orleans. Old Goods will think it perished, and he'll collect the insurance and call himself lucky. I'll be going on to the goldfields. Mr. Moyle here will do what he pleases, and you'll put a few guineas in your own pocket, and who's the wiser for it all?"

"A few *guineas*?" shouted the King. "Are you off your head? We'll be lucky to get pennies for this lot of drivel. What are we to do with *that*?" He pointed at Midgely. "A blind boy! Or with that," he said, jabbing a finger at Boggis. "A great oaf."

So it was true. Midgely and Boggis were to be sold as well. I heard one gasp, and the other groan, and I squeezed Midgely's hand to comfort him.

"You know who takes the risk here," said the King. "Slaving alone is chance enough, but slaving in boys like these—"

"They're convicts, George." Mr. Beezley scratched his leg with the barrel of his gun. "When it comes to telling tales, convicts make dead men look like chatterboxes."

"But still, but still," said the little King, with a despairing glance at his mountain of supplies. "Think of the missus, and the girl. This is all we can afford, and you're stealing us blind."

Mr. Beezley grumbled. He started pulling at the pile of chain, working out the tangles. He raised his voice and asked, "What do you say, Mr. Moyle?"

"Money for old rope," said Mr. Moyle, behind us. "Give us a couple of bodies to carry our goods and call it done."

"Agreed," said the King.

With that we became the property of little King George, and so of Mr. Goodfellow. The very man who had made my life a misery could now do what he liked with the rest of it.

"Oh, don't despair, boys," said the King. "You won't be long on this little island. You'll be off to big plantations; you might fetch up in America. But wherever you go it'll be better than Australia. You won't starve; we promise that. The sugarcane's like lollipops. Work hard, keep your noses clean, and in a few years you'll buy your freedom. Why, you might have slaves of your own one day, if slavery lasts so long."

Mr. Beezley was untangling the pile of chains and shackles. Mr. Moyle went to help him, pulling yards of it loose, until it hung about their shoulders and arms like gruesome garlands.

"We'll do our best to see that you boys stay together," said the little King. "We can't guarantee it. Not every plantation will buy five boys at once."

"*Three* boys, sir," said Walter Weedle, with a funny turn of his head. "Me and Penny, we're staying with Mr. Beezley."

The King scowled at Mr. Beezley. "You're the very devil, sir, aren't you?"

"It's true!" cried Weedle. "Mr. B! Tell him we ain't going as slaves."

"Shut up!" said Mr. Beezley. His arms were full of chains, the gun waving in his hand. "I'm sick to death of hearing from *you,* Captain Kiddy. You toad-eater."

Weedle gaped. He looked so miserable, so suddenly, that I couldn't help but pity him. I thought no boy in the world could possibly look any more dismayed, until I saw Benjamin Penny.

His head was hung down. The lumps of his ears had turned red. All the twisted bones in his shoulders, all the knobs along his back, were heaving and shaking, and a tear splashed onto the dock. He suddenly looked smaller than Midgely, more fragile by half. I remembered the very first time that I'd seen him, and how he'd clung to me in the damp gloom of the Darkey's lair. Mistaking me for my twin, he had shown love and loyalty that I had never seen in him again.

Now he raised his head, and his horrible features were wracked with misery.

"This ain't fair," he said. "You promised, Mr. B."

Mr. Beezley laughed. So did Mr. Moyle. The fifty feet of chain that hung around them jingled with their laughter.

"You're just like all the others," said Penny. "You lie and

cheat; you say one thing and do another. I believed you, Mr. B. I thought you wanted me."

"Wanted *you*?" snorted Mr. Beezley. "Vile little cripple; who'd want *you*? The day I keep the likes of you hanging around me, that's the day I kill myself."

Benjamin Penny gasped. He started forward, over the planks, like a scuttling crab. He uttered every terrible name I'd ever heard, and more. Every name, every curse, and every oath. Then he flung himself at the castaways. He leapt for Mr. Beezley's throat.

His webbed hands clutched on to the man's neck. His feet clawed like a cat's. The gun fell to the dock as Mr. Beezley staggered sideways, shouting in surprise.

Mr. Moyle was right there. He threw loops of chain round Penny's thin neck and tried to strangle him with the links. But the boy hung on, and all three reeled across the dock.

I dashed forward to help Penny. So did Boggis. But in a moment it was all over. Mr. Beezley teetered at the very edge of the dock, with Penny at his throat and Mr. Moyle tugging at the boy. Penny shouted again, and with a twist of his weight he carried the castaways into the sea.

They fell in a tangle and sank straight to the bottom. We could see them, still struggling, on the sand below. A dust—as of gold—swirled around them, growing ever thicker until it covered them over, and only their bubbles of breath could be seen. Three little streams spiraled to the surface, scattered in the currents so that one drifted under the dock. Another faded away, and then the third vanished.

Midgely was shouting, "Tom! Are you there? Tom!"

"It's all right, Midgely," I said.

We all stood gawking into the cloud of sand. The water churned beneath us, as though a great fish was already swooping in beneath the dock. The cloud of sand boiled and raged, and I glimpsed the ghostly shapes of Benjamin Penny and Mr. Beezley embracing each other in a tangle of chain.

Walter Weedle spat into the sea. "Poor old Penny," he said.

It was a shocking sight, made all the worse because it came in gloomy snatches through the shifting cloud of sand. I saw Penny's arm waving as it lifted in the current, Mr. Beezley's ragged beard rippling round his face, his eyes staring open. I felt no pity for the castaways, yet to see little Penny drowned in his chains brought a great pang to my heart. I wondered if it wasn't because of me that he'd come to such a gruesome end.

But I couldn't dwell on it then. Behind me, Midge called out in his soft voice, "Tom, would you help me, please?"

I straightened up and turned around. The little King was there, his face stark white below his woven hat. He was staring at Midgely, who was sitting on the dock with Mr. Beezley's pistol in his hands. The hammer was cocked, the barrel wavering back and forth.

"Tom, where are you?" said Midgely.

"Here," I said, rushing to his side. I took the gun.

I aimed it at the little King.

# *fourteen*
## BENJAMIN PENNY DOES A BRAVE THING

I looked down the barrel of the gun, right into the eyes of King George. He held up his hands, as though to fend off a bullet.

"Please," he said. "Please don't shoot me."

He sank to his knees as I moved toward him. In a moment he was a trembling, tearful sack of jelly. His bearing, his *royalness,* flaked away like old paint. "I beg you," he said. "I've a wife and a child."

I took a step closer.

"I'll give you anything you want," he said. "Name it and it's yours."

"First, your keys." I tried to pull the string over his head, but he grabbed on.

"Be careful now," he said. "If you free the slaves they'll kill you. They'll tear you limb from limb."

"I don't think so." I pulled harder on the string. It snagged on his ear until he finally let go. I gave the keys to Boggis, and sent him off to free the slaves. The pistol I kept aimed at the King.

"Now what?" he said. "Do you want your freedom? You can have it. I'll set you up in New Orleans. In Hispaniola. Wherever you like. You'll have a fine house and so much land that you won't see the edges of it. What do you say, Tom? What do you say to that?"

"I want to go home."

He turned instead to Weedle. "But *you* want it, don't you? Say the word, and freedom's yours. No one will find you, I promise. They won't even go looking; why would they?"

I thought Weedle would now throw himself in with *this* plan, that he'd side with the King as he'd sided with Mr. Mullock and then with the castaways. But to my surprise he only sneered. And to my pleasure he said, "I want to stick with Tom Tin. That's what *I* want from now on."

Midgely smiled at the both of us, or in our general direction. He said, "Is it true, Tom? Is Penny gone?"

"They're all gone," I said. "Penny and Beezley and Moyle."

"Did you see them go down?" asked Midge. "Mr. Beezley ain't coming back, is he?"

"No," I said. "Penny made sure of that."

"It must have been brave of him, then," said Midge.

"Or just stupid," said Weedle. "You could never tell with Penny."

I didn't want to stand there talking about Benjamin Penny. I wanted only to be away, to be out at sea and heading for England. "Let's go home," I said.

"What?" cried the little man. "Right now? At least take us with you." He looked toward his house and that wall of logs, where Boggis was just passing through the opened gate. "Think of the child. Think of her mother. It's their death if you leave us here."

That seemed a possibility. Though I didn't much care what happened to the King, I worried for his little girl.

"You'll need me," said the King. "I can get you home. I know my way around ships, let me tell you. Navigation?" He looked eagerly at me. "I can do it. I can take you right to England."

"Can you take me right to Mr. Goodfellow?" I asked.

I might have knocked him down with a feather. "Now why would you want that?" said he. "Why do *you* care about Mr. Goodfellow?"

"I mean to ruin him," said I. "As he ruined me."

"That's good. That's splendid!" cried the King. "I loathe the man myself. If nothing else, let me help with *that*. With the ruination."

Little King George would surely have said anything then—or promised the moon—to have his wretched life spared. But the tone of his voice, and the look in his eyes, convinced me that he hated Mr. Goodfellow. He went on and on about it, begging for a chance to get even with the man. "I know his habits," he said. "Why, I know the rascal inside out. Believe me, I've suffered for it dearly."

"You don't appear to be suffering," I said. "You trade his slaves, don't you? You were ready to trade *us* a minute ago."

"That's right!" said Weedle, sharply. "He *was*. He should be down there with Mr. Moyle and Mr. B."

"No. No, listen," cried the King. "I've no heart for this business. I really don't. It was Mr. Goodfellow sent me here—to pay my debts, he said. Look, I'm as much a slave as anyone in irons. Why, I'm *more* of a slave than some."

"Push the cove in the water," said Weedle. "You can get us home without him, Tom."

He had more faith in me now than I had in myself. I told the King to get up, for he was still on his knees. I sent him off to fetch his wife and child, and to gather what things they might want for the voyage. "We'll leave while the wind's in our favor," I said.

I didn't even go to shore in that place. I didn't feel the grass below my feet, nor the shade of the trees on my face. I took one more look into the water, where the cloud of sand had nearly settled, and poor Benjamin Penny still lay in the arms of Mr. Beezley. A horde of crabs was already beginning to cover them. As for Mr. Moyle, it was as though he had never existed. Whether the crabs hid him from my view, or whether a shark or a fish had carried him away, I neither knew nor cared.

I threw the King's pistol into the sea. It was heavy and awkward; I didn't trust my aim. So I tossed it from the dock, and it plummeted down in a trail of bubbles, to settle with a puff of golden sand near the head of Mr. Beezley.

"Let's go, Midge," I said, and led him to the ship. The hold had been emptied, and now the slaves were scrubbing it down. In a selfish act I left them to it, only turning them free when the job was done. All but one went off like a shot, leaving a wiry fellow with skin the color of coffee, and a smile as quick as Mercury. In a funny pidgin English he asked to come with us. "Me sail England," he said, making waves in the air with his hand. Then he beamed in that delightful way, and I signed him on with a handshake.

Boggis freed four and twenty slaves. They vanished into the hills like so many deer—with great speed but not a sound. What he saw behind the logs made him more angry than I would have believed to be possible. He came back with his hands swinging like sledgehammers, demanding to know where the King had gone. "I want to thrash him," he growled.

"But, Gaskin, we need him," I said. "He's our navigator now."

It was all that saved the King. But from the instant he came aboard, and for all of our voyage, he would keep as far as he could from Boggis.

I gave him and his family the quarters of our departed castaways. They arrived at the ship in the late afternoon, dragging a coffin down the dock.

The King's wife was a husky woman. She was taller than her husband by a considerable margin, far bigger and stronger as well, though not fat by any means. Loud and brash, it was she who did the dragging, while the King and his tiny daughter pushed from behind. "Put your back in it, George!" she shouted.

It took all of us to hoist that horrible box aboard. I was curious why it weighed so much, but when I bent to the hasp the King's wife laid a meaty hand on the lid. "Please," she said, and suddenly this enormous woman was blushing like a delicate maiden. "My underthings, you understand."

We carried the casket below and left it in the great cabin. The little King, winded already, stayed with it while his wife plodded back for another load as gruesome as the first. I thought we'd brought half the household already, but the second coffin was nearly as heavy as the first.

With the woman at one end, Boggis at the other, and the rest of us in between, we labored the coffin to the break in the deck, where it would spend the entire voyage lashed in place by its handles. Right away the little girl heaved it open, for it turned out that the contents were hers alone. She was surely the only girl with a casket for a playbox, but she didn't mind. It was filled to the brim with her toys and her dolls. Even her tea table came aboard in that grim box.

By the time all was stowed, the sun was setting. Not wishing to make sail in the dark, we decided to lie alongside till morning.

It was a strange night. The birds gave up hunting the flies, but with dusk came a horde of bats. They poured from the trees in a flood, a river of brown swirling through the reddish sky. They flew this way and that, at all heights in all directions, so that it seemed impossible they couldn't help colliding with each other, or with the rigging of the ship. But they darted in and out among the stays and braces, and not a single bat tumbled to the deck.

Then the huts began to burn. It started with a glow of red,

but soon huge flames appeared. They engulfed the buildings, sending embers floating off at great heights above the trees, and the bats and the embers seemed to gather into one enormous, swirling flock.

In the crackle and the roar a chanting started. The slaves were singing—of their freedom, no doubt. They sang all through the night, stoking the flames with the logs from the wooden wall. Midgely and I, and Weedle and Boggis, stood in a row at the rail to listen. I felt my skin prickling down my spine, my hairs standing on end. The sight and the sounds might have come straight from the cannibal islands.

I slept not a wink, but waited anxiously for the dawn. With the first gray of morning's light we loosed the topsails, and the canvas tumbled free. We set the spanker at the stern.

It seemed the ship was mine to command. All eyes were upon me. I put Weedle at the wheel—to please him, more than anything—sent Boggis to the mooring lines, and the others to the sheets and braces. On the dock the British flag flapping from its pole told me of the strength and direction of the wind.

In a small voice I said, "Cast off forward, please."

Away went the lines from the bow. The ship slid backward, squealing and creaking against the dock. Then the stern lines tightened, and the great bowsprit swung away. A gap opened between the bow and the dock, growing wider with each moment.

I felt nearly overwhelmed. The ship seemed unstoppable, already out of control, and we hadn't even parted from the dock. Everyone was staring at me, waiting on my word. But there was such a noise from rope and canvas that I could scarcely think. I heard the little King complaining, then Midgely's answer, clear and loud, "He *does* know what he's doing. His father's the best sailor in the world."

With that I "took the bit in my mouth," as one would say. I shouted at Weedle: "Hard to starboard!" At the others I roared: "Haul away!"

They pulled on the braces, little Midge and the King at one, the woman at the other. Our always-smiling slave tended the spanker. High above, the topsail yards swung over. "Sheet in!" I cried, and the sails filled with wind.

The ship veered faster. It gathered way, sliding forward through the water.

"Cast off aft!" I shouted.

Boggis threw off the last rope, and we were free of the land. We scudded across the bay with the bowsprit sweeping past the trees, past the shore.

"Jibe oh!" I shouted.

The yards came across with a jarring shudder. The spanker boom followed, its blocks in a clatter, its sheets like a whip. Weedle ducked his head as it passed above him, then looked up with a grin.

"Steady as she goes," I told him. He straightened the wheel.

"Set the courses! Set the gallants!"

Our poor little crew scurried from place to place, from braces to sheets. One by one, the sails tumbled free from their yards, each giving the ship another little push to the east. We left the bay with a white-water moustache curling at the bow, flecks of foam in our wake.

I looked down the deck and beyond the bowsprit, at faint hummocks of land in the distance. I didn't know the names of the islands, or a thing about them, but it didn't matter. They marked the edge of the Caribbean, and another day would find us on their far side, with nothing but the broad Atlantic between us and England. It was a daunting thought, all that water to cross, but it no longer filled me with terror.

I should not have looked back, but I did. I saw that half the bay was hidden already, and that only the tip of the pier was still in sight.

I thought of Benjamin Penny, lying drowned in his chains. I thought of the slaves and wondered what would become of them. I imagined that I could see two or three on their knees at the end of the dock, though the distance was surely too great for that. I couldn't help thinking that I'd deserted them, that I'd marooned them in their strange land.

This upset me so much that I sought out Midgely, who always knew just the proper thing to say to set my mind at ease. I found him coiling lines on the leeward side, putting them all in order. The wind had freshened, giving a slant to the deck, so that his ropes lay tight against the rail, and the water leapt not far below us. I told him my fears and worries, but his response was disappointing.

"Do you ever think of Mr. Mullock?" he said. "And that lovely Lucy Beans?"

"Sometimes." I tried to help him with the ropes. But I was "doing it all wrong," he said, as soon as he touched the coil I was making. "With the sun, Tom. Coil 'em with the sun."

I saw what he meant. I'd turned the rope backward, putting kinks in the coil. He let it fall to the deck and started again.

"Do you think Mr. Mullock and Lucy are still happy on their island?" said Midge.

"I'm sure they are," I said.

"But they got nothing," he said. "Mr. Mullock, he had money coming out his ears when he was a lord and all. Now he ain't got tuppence, but he couldn't be happier. He's got Lucy Beans, and that's all he wants. He's living large on his little island, just like he says."

"Then he's fortunate," said I.

Midgely nodded. "It's the same with them slaves, Tom. They ain't got nothing; they're miles from home. But they're happier today than they was yesterday."

Well, that was no doubt true. But I still didn't understand.

"If you could have told them slaves, 'I'll grant you one wish,' what do you think they would have wished for, Tom?"

"To be free, I suppose."

"Well, they are." He hung his coil of rope from a belaying pin and went on to the next. "You gave them the most important thing. It don't matter where they are, so long as they got what they want. That's what I think."

His hands moved steadily, letting the rope fall into place. "If I was one of them slaves I'd thank my saints you came along," he said. "Them slaves ain't slaves no more."

# *fifteen*
## ON A LONG WATCH

We soon settled in to sea-keeping time. Leaving out Midgely, who worked all hours in the galley, we divided ourselves into three watches. Day after day, I was always on deck with the little King and his freed slave, but only rarely with Weedle or Boggis, and hardly ever with the King's wife.

I quickly grew to know my watchmates. I learned that King George was really George King, born near Bethnal Green. For a small man he was a big liar, as we learned not long into the voyage. In truth, he could navigate no better than I.

Oh, he made a show of it, pointing the sextant at the moon and the sun and half of the stars in the heavens. For better than a week I believed he was a master of the strange art, and I might never have learned otherwise if not for his daughter.

Her name was Charlotte—Charlotte King—and she was a darling. The whole ship was her playhouse, with a full complement of imaginary creatures. We were all her toys, her playthings. One moment we were animals in the ark and she was Noah. The next we were pirates and she a young Blackbeard. It meant nothing to us, as we weren't required to play our parts, but merely to stand about as she fed us or stabbed us, according to the rules of the game. Even Walter Weedle was swept up in her play, though always at his expense. In Noah's ark, he was the ass. Over time, Charlotte came to call anything stupid "a weedle."

No one loved that girl more deeply than our slave-turned-sailor. His name was unpronounceable, but Charlotte called him Hay-yoo, because those were the words everyone shouted to get his attention. But to Hay-yoo's dismay, Charlotte saved all her charms for Midgely.

I often found my friend seated at her little table, which they had dragged together into the cookhouse. Midgely spent hours dipping imaginary biscuits into an empty teacup, or sitting grandly still as all the tiny dishes slid back and forth with the rolling of the ship. Sometimes Charlotte would burst into fits of giggles. "Oh, Midgely, you're pouring tea into the cream pot!" she'd shriek.

Midgely didn't mind at all. "Am I? Oh, gracious!" he'd say, and laugh as well.

In the second week of our voyage—it had been three days since I'd seen Walter Weedle—Charlotte came early from her nap time and surprised her father with the sextant. I was steering the ship, and he was standing by the rail, fiddling with the little mirrors and filters, getting ready to shoot the sun. Suddenly he was whisking it behind his back, and Charlotte was clucking her tongue. "Daddy, you're going to be in trouble!" she said.

The King blushed. "Off with you, Charlotte," he told her. "Can't you see we're busy?" He had gone back to his regal ways by then, always referring to himself as "we." But Charlotte never curtsied to the King.

She put her hands on her hips. "Did Mommy say you could use that?"

"Charlotte!" he said, a little more sharply. "We haven't time for this nonsense."

She clucked her tongue again, turned, and went scampering down to the cabins. A moment later she was back, and Mrs. King was with her.

Now *there* was a strange woman. Calliope King—a delicate name for one so strong and manly. She liked to work aloft in her tumbling skirts, with the wind whipping at her pantalettes in the most teasing fashion. Twice the size of her husband, with a voice half an octave deeper, she was more a sailor than any of us, and not only because she chewed tobacco by the plug. Though I fancied I was in command, it was really Calliope King who decided when to reef and when to run, and when to scud before a gale.

She was the daughter of a whaling captain. Born at sea, she'd never touched land until she was nearly five years old. I should have guessed the sextant was hers, and that she was the one who did the navigation—leaning out through the windows at the stern.

Calliope was one who firmly believed that "children should be seen and not heard." She had little to say to Charlotte, and less to any of the boys. She merely kept herself to herself, without being rude about it. I found this made her more interesting, and both Midge and I admired her no end.

But the King lived in fear of his wife, for there was no love between them anymore. I never heard them exchange a kindly word, never saw one even smile at the other. They kept as distant as the ship would allow them. It was no wonder that the King nearly had a fainting spell when Calliope came storming up that day.

She spat a stream of brown juice at his feet, and held out her hand for the sextant. The little King very meekly did as he was directed. He didn't utter a word until she was safely below, when he suddenly found his courage. "What a woman! What a tigress!" he said. "How would you like to have *her* as a mother, Tom Tin?"

I wouldn't have minded. In fact, I'd thought about that very thing. During long turns at the wheel I had amused myself by thinking how different my life might have been if my father had married someone like Calliope. I would have grown up loving the sea instead of fearing it, sharing—not mocking—my father's lonely dreams. But now I had to laugh, for I saw that it would have made no difference in the end. My river of fate would still have brought me to this exact spot—at the wheel of a ship in the middle of the ocean, with Calliope King as the navigator.

So when the little King asked how I'd like to have his

wife as a mother, I thought of many things, and gave a strange answer. "I hope I still *have* a mother."

"What do you mean?" he asked.

"It's a long story," said I.

"It's a long voyage," said he, with a shrug.

I was hesitant to begin my tale. Though I'd come to like the man, he was still a slaver and a liar, not the sort of fellow I cared to trust. I heard a flutter of canvas and looked up to see the wind rippling across the topsail. Without thinking, I turned the wheel to catch the lifting breeze.

"Are you worried that she might be dead?" asked the King.

"Yes," I said, surprised by his bluntness. "She was ill when I left."

"Does she know about the Jolly Stone?" he asked, surprising me again. I couldn't even guess how he'd learned of that.

"Oh, I'm not a wizard," he said, laughing at my astonishment. "I've heard it all through Charlotte. Gaskin told her everything, you know—all about the diamond and the Darkey, and your father and the cannibals."

Boggis, right then, was lumbering across the fo'c'sle deck. He leapfrogged over the capstan with Hay-yoo at his heels, and Charlotte a bit farther behind. They were playing at Gulliver in the land of Lilliput, and it didn't matter that Gulliver was smaller than the Lilliputians.

"I hear your father was Redman Tin," said the King. "Gaskin told Charlotte that he was—"

*"Is,"* I said sharply. "My father *is* Redman Tin, do you

understand? He's still on that island, and he's still alive, and I'll see him again one day. We'll sail together, my father and I."

"Good for you, Tom Tin," said the King. "That's the spirit. Never surrender, what?" He clapped me on the back. "You'll send a ship for him, will you? Dispatch the navy?"

I wasn't certain what I'd do. "Somehow I'll save him," I said. "I'll do what's right by him."

"But first you must win your freedom. Without freedom—"

"I'm always on the run; I know that," I said. "It's the same for Midgely and the others. The Jolly Stone will buy our freedom. It may be cursed, or it may not, but—"

"Oh, it's cursed. There's no doubt about it," said the King. "We've seen the ghost of Captain Jolly looking for his Stone, looking in the moonlight with his phantom ship at anchor in the bay. We've heard him wailing, Tom, and wolves sound happier, let us say."

It was Midgely who'd told me, long ago, about the old pirate, Captain Jolly, and the terrible curse on the diamond. But he hadn't told me—perhaps he hadn't known—that the curse could last beyond death. "Why would his ghost keep looking for the Stone?" I asked.

"To lift the curse," said the King. "Didn't you know—that's the fate for all who've lost it. Those who go to their graves with the Stone unclaimed will walk the earth forever."

It turned me white, the thought of that. I felt a new urgency to unearth the Stone, to pass it on to Mr. Goodfellow. I dreaded that some small accident would befall me first, and that I would spend all of eternity in restless wandering.

"But fear not," said the King. "Old Goods will be only too glad to relieve you of the diamond. Why, that devil—that Old Scratch!—he'd trade his soul to get it, and that's in our favor, Tom. We have the upper hand."

I could see that Boggis must have chattered like a magpie. Through his daughter, the King had learned every detail about how I'd found and lost the Jolly Stone, and he'd worked out a plan that would get me all I wanted. He spelled it out as the ship hurdled the waves toward England, as Charlotte and the giant Lilliputians raced across the fo'c'sle deck.

"Here's what we'll do," he said. "The moment we land, we must seek out Mr. Goodfellow."

"Do you mean you and I?"

He shook his head. Impatiently, he gave up his royal "we," jabbing a finger at my chest, and then at his. "*You'll* go off and get the diamond. *I'll* find Mr. Goodfellow and bring him to the ship. I'll help you barter a trade. Remember, Tom, I know that devil's way of business. I can drive him to his knees."

"What would you want in return?" I asked.

"Nothing!" said he, as though it was an insult to ask. "Only that the diamond brings a curse to that monster. He took away my comfort and my future as he took away yours, and it's all I want to see him suffer."

It was part of the curse that I'd be suspicious. The King might have been trying, like everyone else, to feather his own nest. But there was certainly no pretense in his hatred for Mr. Goodfellow. If anything, it was deeper than my own. He held out his hand on the bargain, and I shook it.

"Here's to the end of Mr. Goodfellow," he said.

I felt relieved to be sharing my burden, glad that time and sea miles had made a shipmate from this pudgy man I'd so detested. I looked at the sails, at the compass, and gave the wheel a quarter turn.

Up by the bow, Charlotte's hair was like a splash of sunlight. She was sneaking round the capstan, not knowing that Hay-yoo was waiting to pounce.

"Look at her. What innocence," said the King. "She was never afraid of the natives, you know. I was terrified, let me tell you. Dead within a week, I thought. Slaughtered in our beds. But Charlotte charmed them like a songbird."

We watched the girl creep around the capstan. With a shout, Hay-yoo leapt out at her, his arms held up like a lion's paws. Charlotte shrieked happily, and raced off in the other direction as Boggis tried to grab her.

The King laughed heartily. "He was always a fine fellow, that Hay-yoo. Almost a nanny to Charlotte." He looked at me, then looked away. "Do you know, between you and me and the gatepost, Tom, I don't believe there's much difference between ourselves and the savages. It's almost heresy to say so, but watch them with Charlotte and you see. They're pleasant and friendly, and some are sharp as tacks. It's a curious thing, Tom. Free a slave, and you've a friend for life."

"You told me they'd murder us all if I set them free," I said.

"Of course I *told* you that. My livelihood was about to vanish," he said, with a toss of his hand. "Setting the slaves loose was like throwing guineas into the forest. But do you know, I'm glad to be out of it, Tom. There's no future in slaving."

"It's illegal," I said.

"In England, yes. That's just what I mean," said he. "The whole business is doomed. Like the quill pen and the flintlock, slavery's had its day. Why not, when you think about it? There's steam engines now, and plenty of others to do the work. You've got your convicts and your lunatics and your children. Why go to all the trouble of gathering slaves and carting them from hither to yon?"

He said all this very pleasantly, as though there was nothing wrong with the notion that slavery was his right and his due. I thought I would despise any man who thought such a thing, but I didn't feel any hatred. To my surprise, I found I'd become rather fond of George King.

"How did you become a slaver?" I asked. "What happened between you and Mr. Goodfellow?"

He didn't answer right away. The ship moved along in its watery rumble, with the creaks of rope and wood, and I thought he wouldn't answer at all. Then he sighed.

"It was the wife's fault, Tom." The King turned his back and spoke into the wind. "You see, we used to carry passengers to the Orient in an Indiaman, I as chief steward—and a damned good one—and she as the captain. When Charlotte was born we settled ashore. I went to work for Mr. Goodfellow, overseeing his office boys. Well, just last year—or was it the year before?—he ventured into the slaving trade. He tried to make me twist the wife's arm so that she'd command one of his ships. I told him I'd rather twist a lion's tail."

The King laughed to himself. "Mr. Goodfellow tried the twisting himself, and you know the long and short of it, Tom. Much the same thing happened to your father. No one crosses old Goods without suffering for it, and isn't that the truth? Within a month we were penniless. Within two we owed our souls to Mr. Goodfellow, and he packed us off to the slaving station. It was that, or be out on the streets. The wife would have chosen the streets if not for Charlotte."

The King fell silent. We stood rather awkwardly, with nothing more to say, and no easy way to move apart. We both watched the sea, on opposite sides of the ship, until Charlotte scampered down the deck toward us. The King ventured another remark. "She takes all her games so seriously."

Charlotte came skipping to the quarterdeck. "Daddy!" she cried. "Come and help me feed my dollies. We can feed Mr. Horrible too."

The King laughed. "That's her imaginary friend," he said to me, taking her hand.

"He's *not* imaginary," said Charlotte. "He's real."

"Yes, of course he is." The King winked at me as she pulled him away. "What a weedle you have for a father."

They left me alone at the wheel. I felt the slant of the deck and the pull of the ship, and I heard the wind's song in the rigging. A sense of contentment came over me at the thought that I had found an ally.

I should never have forgotten that the King was a liar.

# sixteen
## THE GIRL AND MR. HORRIBLE

Watch followed watch, and day followed day. Two thousand miles or more we sailed, and while I was thrice laid flat by sickness, I was never once scared. Mrs. King charted us past the Azores and on toward England. Then she called us all on deck one morning and told us to watch for land.

It was the first time we'd all been together since we'd weathered a storm in mid-Atlantic. Weedle looked changed, as indeed he was. Without Penny around him, he was cheerful—even friendly—and the voyage had made him a happier person. His scar would always give an evil twist to his face, but behind it, somehow, he was smiling.

Boggis went aloft, Weedle to the wheel, and we all watched for England.

Poor Midgely could not be included in our eager lookout. But he smelled land before any of us could see it, and he hauled me to the rail, pointing at an empty sea. "Look harder! Look harder!" he cried.

High above me, Gaskin Boggis hopped to his feet on the topsail yard. He jumped up and down on that wooden stick, shouting, "Land! There's land!"

Mrs. King, her cheek bulging with tobacco, flew straight to the rigging. It was a boisterous day, and her skirts, catching the wind, bulged like a bell around her white drawers. "It's the Lizard!" she said.

To me it was a faint speck of gray, a shard of rock that could have been anything anywhere. How I envied that she could name it, as if she had an acquaintance with every stone and sod of the earth.

She squirted tobacco juice neatly between the shrouds. "A point to leeward, please," she shouted down at the wheel.

Weedle hesitated, jogging the wheel one way, then the other.

From Charlotte came her tongue-clucking. "Leeward means to leeward, you weedle." She pointed toward the land. "Silly goose; turn that way."

We passed the Lizard and ran down the Channel. With the wind in our favor, but the tide against us, we bashed through row after row of steep-sided waves. The very ship trembled, and the spray flew up from the bow.

My home looked cold and dismal, an uninviting place. It was a disappointment after the grand vision I'd been imagining for so long. But when Midgely asked me to describe it, I said it looked beautiful.

All day and all night we pressed along the Channel. Weedle and Boggis and Hay-yoo stood staring into the night. We all saw the lights of Dover in the darkness, the twinkle of thousands of candles and lamps. A strange feeling came over me, like the queasy sense of the seasickness. I'd thought I would be overjoyed to be home, but now I wished that I had another day, or another week, at sea. I was suddenly not sure that I wanted to go home at all.

The King asked me, "What's on your mind, Tom?"

"I couldn't really say," I told him. "I think I'm afraid of facing Mr. Goodfellow again. Things might go badly for me."

"Nonsense, Tom," he said. "We'll watch over you like your own guardian angel."

We gave the Goodwin Sands a wide berth in the darkness, and sighted the Foreland at dawn. Like birds woken by the sun, a flock of boats came flying out from shore. In the distance they were little clouds of foam and spray, for they came with all sails set, racing each other to be first alongside.

They tacked and jibed, their hulls vanishing wholly into the seas. They shot past our bow and tore round the stern, a man calling from each, "Pilot! Pilot!"

Mrs. King chased them off. She said there was no need to lug a man "all over the blooming ocean," and that we would pick up our pilot when we'd rounded the Foreland.

We did that at noon. We passed the point two miles off, turned to the west, and braced the yards for a reach toward the river. There, at the mouth of the Thames, we found a bulge of brown water—a huge bubble on the blue of the North Sea. I felt a change in the ship as we punctured that bulge, crossing from blue to brown, from salt to fresh. As though from a wish to head back to the ocean, the ship slowed and veered aside, so that Boggis had to fight it with the wheel.

Then, two miles from any shore, I put down Midgely's bucket and scooped fresh water from the sea.

The little King grimaced when he saw me lift it to my lips. "You're not drinking *that,* are you?" he said.

It was river water, fouled with sewage, thickened by mud from the fields. I would not have drunk it for love nor money when I lived in London. But now, at the edge of the sea, it was somehow different. I fancied that I could smell all of its parts: the rain that fell on the lovely Cotswold Hills; the spray of the Temple Fountain; the bathwater of the King in his castle; the runoff from the coppery dome of St. Paul's.

"It's the blood of England," I said. It was her essence, a potion of courage and strength.

I tipped the bucket and drank. Then Boggis pulled it away and did the same, and the bucket went from hand to hand, from mouth to mouth, sloshing over the deck as we all drank of England's blood.

With the current against us, and the river chopping at our bow, Calliope King finally allowed a pilot aboard. He clambered up the same ladder that had saved our loathsome castaways, that had rescued Midgely and me and the others.

He was a grizzled old salt, bundled head to toe in his heavy cloak. He went straight to the wheel and rooted himself behind it, where the deck was spotted from Calliope's tobacco. Only inches from the helmsman, he bellowed orders at the top of his lungs. "Larboard! Larboard! Come about!"

I thought I would stand on the deck and not move until I saw the spires of London, until I heard the bells in the churches. But our progress was terribly slow, and it wasn't until the next morning that the land began to narrow around us. We passed the mouth of the Medway, and I remembered my terror as I'd sailed out from there in the hold of my father's ship, a convict on my way to Australia. I looked toward Chatham for the short masts of the hulks, but saw nothing but marshes and hills.

Below the Beacon Hill, near the village where I was born, the land pressed close on either side. The pilot took us up with the tides, tacking back and forth. We sailed so close to the river's edge that we could see the grasses bending in the wind, and twice we startled herons into flight. At each change to the ebb he dropped the anchor, and we waited for the current to turn again in our favor. There were times we gained fewer than five miles, when the flood was weak.

The long hours of waiting gave us time to think and time to talk. No longer divided by watches, we could gather as we pleased. One night, as we sat out the ebbing tide, Weedle and Boggis and Midgely and I were together in the cookhouse. There was a touch of moonlight on the marshes, and I was looking out the window when Weedle began to pester me with questions.

"What will happen when we get to London?" he said. "First thing, what will we do?" He was sitting with his back to the wall, picking at a spot of tar on his trousers. "Will we give a cove a tumble? Pick a pocket?"

"No," I said.

"We have to get money somehow, don't we? Then we'll buy roasted chestnuts. And ices and muffins. That's what we want to do, ain't it, Gaskin?"

Boggis shook his head.

"What then?" said Weedle. "Do we go straight off to Cheapstreet?"

I looked down at him. "You can go wherever you like, but not straight off," I said. "You'll stay on the ship while I go ashore and—"

"Stuff that!" Weedle jumped up. "Why should *you* go ashore and not us?"

"'Cause that's the way it is," said Midgely, glaring blindly at the place where Weedle had sat. "He's going to get pardons for us all. Ain't that right, Tom?"

"You stupid toadie!" shouted Weedle. "What makes you think he'll come back? To help *you*? A blind boy? He can run faster and farther without you."

The sudden argument left me disheartened. Through all we'd done and all we'd seen, had it been only to end as we'd started, in squabbling and shouting? I turned to leave the cookhouse.

"Where are you going?" cried Weedle. "Tom, wait!"

It seemed he thought I would go ashore right then, swimming through the river, crawling through the marshes. He grabbed my shirt, and in a desperate voice begged me not to go.

"You brought us all the way here, you have to look out for us," he said. "There ain't no one else. I ain't got Penny or Carrots or no one no more. You got to look out for me, Tom."

It was a wretched display. Weedle was so afraid of being abandoned that he came close to tears. Then shame alone made it worse, and when his voice began to blubber he pushed past me, running out into the dark.

Boggis heaved himself up. "I better go talk to him," he said. "I don't like people being sad."

If Boggis had his own fears, he kept them to himself. But if he didn't, he would have been the only one. The farther we went up the river, the more Midgely fretted. He thought of his mother in the dockyard, but couldn't decide if he should go to her. "She turfed me out once," he said. "Don't know why she'd want me back now."

Around our ship gathered barges and frigates and cutters and snows, all making their way with the tides, like a strange sort of city drifting upriver. Now and then a beautiful ship would go gliding right past us, pulled by a filthy steam tug with its side-paddles churning.

There was no end of things to see, and for most of us that slow week on the river was endlessly exciting. We shouted back and forth with bargemen and boatmen. We gazed at people on the shore. The wiry Hay-yoo looked out on the villages and churches with the same astonishment I'd shown at the sight of jungles. Midgely never complained that he couldn't see the wondrous things, but I found him constantly rubbing his eyes, as though he could squeeze out his blindness.

Charlotte was in her element, playing at counting sheep and counting birds and counting barges. She made little boats that she launched from the stern, and sometimes they went sailing past us. Her laugh seemed to fill the ship.

"Is she pretty?" asked Midgely, as we passed the steamship dock at Greenwich pier.

"Very much," I told him.

"I thought so." He nodded. "She *sounds* pretty, Tom. She sounds even more pretty than Lucy Beans. Angels must sound like Charlotte."

We were getting close to the City. The air was thickening with the smells of smoke and river stench. Marshes had given way to docks and buildings. But Midge sat wrapped in his darkness while a troop of dragoons rode by at a trot, while a toff in a top hat went weaving past on his two-wheeled dandy horse, pushing along with his feet.

"She plays such funny games," he said. "Has she told you about Mr. Horrible, Tom?"

"Not really," I said. "I heard her say the name, that's all."

"She told *me* all about him," he said, with a proud smile. "Every day she asks me for a bit of food for Mr. Horrible. She says he lives below, in a box in the steerage. No one ever sees him."

"Is he invisible?" I asked.

"No, don't be silly!" cried Midge, with a bright laugh. "His door's locked, Tom; that's all. Charlotte comes for bits of beef or the fat from the mutton. She says that's his favorite 'cause he doesn't have to chew it. I think she pitches it over the side, or gives it to Calliope. But she always says thank you. Like that. 'Thank you, Midgely.' That's why I think she's so pretty."

I hadn't realized that he'd become so besotted by the girl. It was really no wonder, for she was delightful, a little blond elf flitting through the ship. She'd kept us all laughing our way up the river.

"It makes me sad I'll never see Charlotte," said Midge. "But you know what makes me sadder? I'm forgetting what *you* look like, Tom." He tipped his face toward me, and his eyes were nearly closed. "I try to remember, but I can't. I'm forgetting what you look like, and—you know something?—I'm forgetting what *I* look like too. It's funny, ain't it? But I must be all right, 'cause Charlotte seems to like me."

We passed the domes of the naval college, and the big docks at Greenland and Millwall. We saw the masts of tall ships in Limehouse Basin. Then, at last, we sighted St. Paul's, and the cross at the top of its dome. That evening we anchored off the grim Tower, and I had come full circle. It was near this very place that I had pulled my diamond from the river mud and fled with the blind man on my heels.

In the morning, Hay-yoo was gone. We supposed he'd swum ashore to the Tower Stairs, slipping into the huge city as though into a jungle. Charlotte wept, and even the King had to dab his eyes with his handkerchief. Calliope said a little prayer for the soul of Hay-yoo, as though he'd been buried at sea. Then we pressed on, and the next day found us high in the Pool. The arches of London Bridge blocked the river ahead, and all around was a confusion of construction. We had gone as far as we could go.

# seventeen
## I LEAVE MIDGELY BEHIND

Around the Pool, buildings rose sheer from the river in cliffs of stone and brick. Here and there were iron moorings set into the walls, and we made fast to a pair of great rings. Out from the water, up the wall, rose a metal ladder black with rust, dangling seaweed and branches from every rung.

The pilot wasted no time. As soon as our ropes were fastened he called for a boatman, then gathered his charts and his sea boots, stuffed his hat into his pocket, and stood by the rail. I begged a ride with him, so that I might strike out straightaway for my old home.

"What, you too?" he said. "Good crikey, I should have called for a barge; that's three of you now. Well, look lively. My boat's on the way."

Calliope and Charlotte were bustling about, filling the dreadful playbox with the girl's many things. I said a quick good-bye to Gaskin and Weedle. "I'll be back in the morning," I said. "Whatever you do, don't leave the ship."

"We won't," said Boggis, while Weedle shook his head solemnly. "Hurry back, Tom."

Next, I shook hands with the little King. He looked unusually sad. "You're not going ashore?" I asked.

"Oh, we've been forbidden," he said, with a rueful look. "Calliope wants everything in order first. Honestly, I'm glad for some peace from that woman."

"Have you told her about the Jolly Stone?" I asked.

"Of course not," said he. "Believe me, I've done my best to keep Calliope in the dark, though I fear she may have gotten wind of it." He motioned me closer, and his voice fell to a whisper. "Now don't breathe a word of this, Tom—not to her, and especially not to Charlotte—but I believe we've come to a parting of the ways. When we're through with Mr. Goodfellow, I'll go about a landsman's business, and leave the sea to Calliope. Poor old sea."

He was trying to be cheerful, but not succeeding. Finally, he sent me off with a pat on the back. "Remember, Tom," he told me. "Bring the diamond here an hour after dawn. I'll have Mr. Goodfellow waiting. That will be a nice touch, won't it? *Him* waiting for *you*?"

Last, I said so long to Midgely. He came out of the cookhouse, and, holding my sleeve, walked toward the ladder. The pilot was leaning on the rail, watching his boatman row across the Pool. The little white boat was dodging barges and lighters.

"Can't you take me, Tom?" said Midge. "I don't want to stay here with Weedle and the King. I got a funny feeling, Tom."

"I have to go alone," I said.

"Please?"

"Midge, no! You're too small, and you're too slow."

I spoke so sharply that the pilot turned and looked at me. Midgely let go of my sleeve, and his lip began to quiver. "Please, Tom," he said. "I can run."

"No," I told him. "I've a long way to walk, Midge; I can't carry you. Oh, Lord, you don't *see!*"

What I meant was *You don't see what I'm saying; you don't understand.* But Midge began to cry, and the pilot swore at me. "What a terrible thing to say to a blind boy."

Midgely, sniffing, smeared the back of his hand across his nose. "That's something Weedle would say. Or Benjamin Penny. I know I can't see; you don't have to tell me."

"Midge, I'm sorry." I tried to touch him, but now *he* pulled away from *me*.

"Go on then, Tom," he said. "I don't care figs what you do."

I had no chance to explain. Calliope and Charlotte came dragging the coffin full of toys. The boatman, just then clambering to the deck, stopped with one foot on the rail. "No!" he cried. "Not in my boat, you don't. You're not taking a dead man in *my* boat."

Calliope spat a brown river. "It's only toys, you idiot," she said. "But there'll be a dead man soon enough if you don't give me a hand."

She was not a woman to be argued with. The boatman—and the pilot too—were quick to obey. The coffin was more than half the length of the boat, so they laid it sideways across the stern, and Calliope sat atop it. "Hurry up, Charlotte," she said.

The girl was holding hands with Midgely. It seemed she had just discovered that he was crying. "What's the matter?" she said. "Why are you so sad, Midgely? Are you going to miss me that much?"

He only nodded, too teary to speak.

"You're sweet, Midgely," she said. "Will you do something for me? Will you feed Mr. Horrible?"

He nodded. "Of course," he said, as though he'd never had a thought for anything else.

"Don't forget now. If you're frightened, just slide it under his door." She squeezed his hands. "He's not really so horrible. Just a bit of a weedle. Stinky too."

"Oh, I don't mind," said Midge. He raised his voice, to be sure I would hear. "I'm used to stinky fellows by now."

Charlotte giggled. "You're funny, Midgely. I shall miss you. I shall miss you dearly." Suddenly she leaned forward and kissed his cheek.

Midge turned red and couldn't talk anymore. He just stood there as Charlotte slipped down to the boat.

"I'll be back before dawn," I told Midge, but he gave no answer.

The boatman ferried Calliope and Charlotte to the nearest steps. He balanced the boat with his oars as Calliope heaved the coffin ashore.

"Tom, I wish you were staying with the ship," she said. "At least until I return. It would be safer all around. The city's a dangerous place."

Well, it was too late for me to stay with the ship, and she didn't have a chance to tell me more. The boatman was already shouting at me to "Shut up and sit still," already pushing off into the river. So I only waved good-bye to the girl and her mother, until I was told to stop that as well. "You're fanning the air," said the boatman, with a curse.

On I went with the pilot. The tide was in our favor, bearing us swiftly under the bridge, past the new one in the making. A strong current made for a lazy boatman, and ours only steered with his oars. "Where have you been in your ship, sonny?" he asked, turning his head. I said I had gone nearly to Australia and back, that I'd been beyond the seas, by way of cannibal islands and the Caribbean.

"Well, that's a start," he grunted. "Perhaps one day you'll be able to manage the Thames."

I rode as far as the pilot was bound—to Blackfriars Bridge. From there I went by foot, up St. Bride's and through the busy whirl of Holborn Circle. The street sweepers didn't bother to sweep for me. The sellers of boiled puddings and crumpets and gingerbread nuts didn't cry out as I passed. I must have been a strange sight: a boy in salt-stained sailor's clothes rushing through the streets.

I came out at Hatton Garden, where the jewelers had their shops. In the windows that I passed were rows of little diamonds that would have blushed with shame if mine had been set amongst them. The wonderful Jolly Stone would have looked like the full moon against a sky of tiny stars.

I saw a jeweler stooped at his counter, peering through a thing that looked like the stubbed end of a spyglass. On impulse I went into his shop.

He was leaning forward with his elbows on the counter, studying a diamond not half the size of a pea. He turned it round and round in his fingers.

When I coughed to get his attention he let the glass drop from his eye, catching it neatly in his palm. Then he smiled at me, very kindly, with a twinkle as bright as his diamond. "Yes?" he said.

I shaped my hand as though it held my Jolly Stone. "What would it be worth, sir? A diamond as big as this?"

He gaped, as I'd expected he would. But then he laughed. "Get away! You're pulling my leg."

"I'm not, sir," I said. "I found one like that. Or, rather, I found it and lost it, and now I'm about to find it again."

He looked doubtful. "How big do you say?"

I shaped my fist again. He squinted at it, then bent down and rummaged in the boxes below his counter. He popped up for another look, dropped down again, and finally rose with something cupped in his hands. "Is this what your diamond's like?"

I glimpsed something shiny as his fingers spread slowly apart, like an oyster revealing its pearl. Then the light from the windows caught that thing, and flashed back at my face from the shadows of his palms. It was very much like my Jolly Stone, but so pure that it was nearly transparent. It absorbed the colors of his skin and cast them back threefold in bands as bright as fire.

"Is this what you found?" he said. "Something like this?"

"Yes, sir. Very much like that," I said. "What would you say if I brought you another?"

At last he opened his hands completely. "I'd say you nicked your mother's doorknob, son," he said. For that was exactly what he placed on the counter; not my *mother*'s door-knob, but a doorknob nonetheless.

"No," I said. Into my mind came words I'd nearly forgot-ten, an image of a lawyer in Newgate Prison. *"It will turn out to be a broken bottle, a bit of shiny glass."*

I hadn't trusted the lawyer then, and I didn't want to be-lieve the jeweler now. "You're wrong," I said. "It *was* a dia-mond I found. It was the Jolly Stone."

"Ah, the good old Jolly Stone," he said, as happily as ever. "That old chestnut." His eyes kept their twinkle, but the smile was replaced by a look of pity. "It's only a story, son. Only a fancy."

"It's more than that," I said. "It *must* be more than that."

"Well, perhaps you're right," he said. "In a sense I hope you are. But in a sense I hope you're not, for even the small-est diamond holds more misery than bears to be thought about. They're *made* of misery, I think. Cast in the colors of tears and blood. If you find that stone, and it turns out to be real, don't bring it to me, I beg you."

I looked into his eyes for some sign that he was only try-ing to lead me on, to steal my treasure in the end. But he looked right back with nothing but kindness. So I left his shop and carried on, wishing I'd never gone in.

Through the city and into country, I kept seeing in my mind the jeweler's doorknob shining in his hands. I couldn't have traveled the breadth of the world and back, and suffered the things I'd suffered, all for a piece of glass. The idea was too cruel to be possible.

But it plagued me through the streets, past the fields and the burying grounds. It consumed me, so that I wasn't aware of the gathering night until I looked up and saw the stars and the bright, full moon. They might have been there to mock me.

I had reached the corner of the street where I'd lived. I counted the doors as I passed them, for the wretched places were all alike. Then I stopped at the one I had come out from a year before.

I paused before I opened it, scared of what I'd find.

# *eighteen*
# A SAD HOMECOMING

The place was dark but not empty. A spray of light came through the bottom of the door, painting yellow on the crooked porch and the tips of my boots.

I raised my hand to knock, then tested the door instead. It swung open at a touch.

Inside, all was the same, but all was different. I could see the sideboard and the sofa that we'd brought in the drayman's cart, the glass-fronted cabinet where my father had displayed his keepsakes. The same carpet was on the floor.

But the cabinet was full of figurines I'd never seen, and on the sideboard sat many small ornaments that were strange to my eyes. In the place of our old armchair was a fine divan covered with a crimson plush.

It seemed my mother had come up a step in the world. I felt relief and happiness, but a prick of pain as well. It hurt me to think that she was better off without me.

I let the door click shut. I called through the darkness, into the light of the kitchen. "Mother, I'm home!"

"Who's that?" was the answer. Even her voice had changed.

"It's me. It's Tom," I said.

I heard a chair shift on the floor, and then footsteps. Into the doorway came an utter stranger, a woman with a craggy face, like an old statue that had come to life.

"You must be looking for Mrs. Tin," she said.

"Yes, I'm her son," said I.

"Well, a fine son *you* are, showing up at the door eight months since she's gone."

"Gone?" I said. "Where's she gone to, miss?"

"To her *great reward,*" she said, with a snorting little laugh. "No one but the doctor to hold her hand. You should be ashamed of yourself! Where were you, you scamp? Down in the City, I suppose. Making merry, or making mischief, if it ain't one and the same."

I shook my head, but didn't answer. I'd been nowhere near the City then. I'd been in the hold of my father's transport ship, sailing to Australia. It had been about that time that he'd had his vision of my mother appearing by his bedside in the Southern Ocean.

"So why have you shown up *now*?" asked the craggy woman. "If you think it's to claim her belongings, you've got another think coming. I paid for them outright, all legal with lawyers. It wasn't she what owned them at any rate."

"I know. It was Mr. Goodfellow," I said.

"Yes, that's a fact." She looked into the front room, as though to see if I'd disturbed it. Her nose cast a long shadow on the wall. "So now you can pack yourself off again, boy," she said. "Quick! Before I call for the Charlie."

I went without another word, and in utter dismay I retraced my steps to the City. Suddenly I was motherless—perhaps an orphan, though I wouldn't allow myself to think of *that*. I felt that I ought to cry for my mother, but try as I might I couldn't feel much sorrow. I barely remembered the mother I had loved more than anything. That one had died years before, replaced by the black shell of a woman who'd been turned to madness by my sister's death. I remembered the last words she had spoken to me: *"I have no son."*

She had begged me to stay, I remembered. Like Midgely, she had grabbed hold of me and tried to stop me from leaving. She must have waited for me, and waited for Father. She must have spent all her days and nights at the window. I could imagine her there, a woman in black, in candlelight, staring out at a world as dark as her shawls.

I'd abandoned my mother in a lonely house, my father on a cannibal island. Did I leave both of them wondering if I'd ever come back?

It was all too much to bear. In a lonely churchyard I stopped and sat on the ground. In moments I was in tears, sobbing away beneath the stars and the gravestones. Chilled to the bone, frightened and lonely, I wished that someone would save me.

Of course no one came. I cried what tears I had, and slowly my sadness was replaced by rage. I blamed Mr.

Goodfellow for everything that had happened. It was he who'd brought about the death of my mother and the loss of my father, he who was responsible for my own sorry state right then. I had set out months ago to "settle accounts" with Mr. Goodfellow. I could see now that the debit side had grown much longer. So up I got, and squared my shoulders, and marched off to see the business through.

By the time I reached the river I'd traveled nearly twenty miles, most of it on foot. I'd hopped on the back of a hackney coach, until a silly toff had cried out to the driver, "I say! You've got a passenger there, you know." All I'd eaten were a few windfall apples, brown and mushy, that I'd found by the road. But I couldn't stop, for I had only until dawn to find my diamond and take it to the ship.

I tramped wearily along the streets to the north of the Tower. I must have crossed the path I'd taken with old Worms, but nothing looked familiar. I listened for the rattle of his wagon, for the strange clomp of his three-legged horse. But there was nothing to help me. Even the verses I thought I'd committed to memory, the clues I'd thought so clever, had vanished from my mind.

To add to my trouble, there was a whiff of sulfur in the air, the first sign that the yellow fog would soon be thick around me. A thin dusting of coal from the thousands of fires lay on my shoulders already.

The streets teemed with people and horses and carts and curricles. Slowly they emptied as the night went on. But they were never deserted. As the last of the gentlemen and ladies and costermongers vanished, the first of the scavengers appeared. Soon there was an army of them skulking through the streets, searching out cigar ends, tipping over dustbins, scraping up the droppings of horses and dogs.

Round and round I wandered, trying to remember my verses. I recalled a wooden boot and the Tyburn route, and a sewer drain somewhere. When I came across a blacking house I remembered very clearly how Worms had turned left after passing such an establishment. But now, when I did the same, it only led me to *another* blacking house, and left me more lost than ever.

I wished I were more like Midgely, who seemed to remember every single word that every soul had spoken to him. I wished for that and . . . I stopped dead in my tracks. I had told him the verses! I remembered very clearly lying beside him in the hulk, swinging in our hammocks. I had recounted those forgotten lines to keep them planted in my mind. There was a fair chance that he would remember them still. Why, it was better than fair! He might recall them word for word.

I ran to the river, not stopping until I reached the rusted ladder where our ship had tied up. From its top I looked down—at nothing but empty water. I leaned out, dizzied by the height and the swirling eddies below me. I could scarcely believe it, but the ship was gone.

My first thought was that the old thing had given up the ghost, that—reaching land at last—it had let go of its moorings and eased to a rest in the river mud. But the Thames was not deep enough to hide its masts, and so I gazed across the Pool. There were many vessels, large and small, and a floating forest of masts. There among them, in the gloomy shadows of the buildings, was my old ship, tied alongside a wharf.

Even from where I stood it looked deserted, like a ghost ship in the river. It *felt* deserted when I finally stepped aboard, in the hour before the dawn.

I called for Midgely, but there was no answer. I went straight to the cookhouse, only to find it empty. The little blanket that Midgely had drawn over himself every night was cast into a corner. His mug full of spoons and knives had been tipped from the table, covering the deck with cutlery that clanged and tingled as I walked.

"Midge?" I said, stupidly. He wasn't there; it was plain to see. No one was there. But why?

It was easy to imagine Weedle and Boggis lured away by the city. What a hard task I'd given them to stand surrounded by all the bustle of London, and to do no more than look at it. It would have been more of a wonder if they *hadn't* gone ashore.

But I couldn't believe Midgely would have gone with them. I had left him angry and hurt, but still . . . I was certain he would have waited for me.

I went to the stern and down to the cabins, to the part of the ship I hadn't seen since our earliest fears of ghosts and hauntings. It was tidy and clean, with such a fussiness about it that I was certain King George—and not Calliope—had done the cleaning.

I looked in every cabin, in every space. The door to the steerage was open, and inside was the second coffin, emptied of whatever had been carried inside it. Other than that, there was little doubt that this was the home of Charlotte's imaginary Mr. Horrible. The space had been hurriedly cleaned, but bits of food were still scattered around it, some fresh and some moldy.

The ship was truly deserted. It had the same sad feeling that I remembered from our first day aboard. To stand on the empty deck, even in the crowded Pool of London, was an eerie sensation. It was as though the ship had rid itself of every soul, and hauled itself alongside to collect another ghostly cargo.

I went back to the cookhouse and stared at Midgely's crumpled little blanket. It seemed such a pathetic thing, and such a mystery all around me. I was trying to make sense of it when I heard my name being shouted, and turned to see King George hurrying up the gangway.

He was wearing the breeches again that made his legs look like fat drumsticks. He came toward the cookhouse.

"Have you got it?" he said. "The diamond, Tom; have you got it?"

I didn't care tuppence for the diamond just then. "Where's Midge?" I demanded. "Where's Weedle and Gaskin?"

"Oh, Tom, there's bad news."

The King stepped over the high sill, into the cookhouse. It was then the time between darkness and dawn, when the world was shades of gray. The air stank of the brewing fog.

"Soldiers came," said the King. "Whole troops of them, Tom. A regiment, maybe. They had the ship moved over here to the dock. Then they took away Weedle and Gaskin in chains, and—oh!—how that big one struggled. He took three of them down before they got him."

"What about Midge?" I asked.

"No, they didn't take Midgely."

"Then where is he?"

"Oh, somewhere safe and sound. Don't worry," said the King. "He was taken away."

"What do you mean?" I asked. "Who took him?"

"Hang on, Tom." The King tugged at his breeches. "Let's start at the beginning. You do have the diamond, don't you?"

"I don't," I said, angered that we were already back to the diamond.

"Why not?"

"I can't find it without Midgely."

"Oh, crikey!" said the King. "There's a turn-up for the books. There's a sticky wicket." He fell into a chair at the table. "Here, you're the one who buried the Stone; why can't you go back to the same place?"

"I don't know where the place *is,*" I said. "It's a year since I saw it, and I was lost in the fog. I've forgotten how to get back. But I told Midge, and he'll remember."

"You're certain you can't find it on your own?"

"I could," I said. "No, I *would*—if I had enough time. But it might take hours. It might take days. I'd have to blunder around for—"

"Well, go and blunder!" said the King. "For heaven's sake, we need that Stone before we bargain with Mr. Goodfellow."

I looked suspiciously at the little man. "He's supposed to

meet us here at *dawn,*" I said. "Did you keep your part of the bargain? Did you go to see him?"

"Oh, Tom!" The King laughed, but it sounded false. "Goods warned of this, don't you know. He said you're a sharp one. 'Watch for Tom; he's a sharp one.' That's what he said."

"What else did he say?" I asked.

"Well, he refused to come to the ship. Flat out refused," said the King. " 'Send the boy to me.' Those were his words. 'Send that scamp to me.' He asked if there was something you valued more than any other, and we said, 'That would be Midgely.' "

"Why did you tell him that?"

"It's called bargaining," the King said grandly. "We were playing our cards close to our vest."

"Bargaining? That's called stupid," I said. "He came and took Midge!"

"Ah, that's what he *thought* he would do." The King held up a finger. "But we outwitted him, Tom."

Word by word the tale unfolded. The King didn't look at me, but glanced often through the doorway as dawn brought to the sky the awful, yellow light of London's fog.

"Mr. Goodfellow's no fool," he said. "He wouldn't trust you to hand over the diamond, so he wanted something up his sleeve. He thought he would hold something of yours for ransom. But worry not." Red in the face from all his talking, the King leaned back in his chair. "We have the upper hand, Tom."

"How's that?" The story didn't seem to quite hang together. "Just how did you outwit Mr. Goodfellow?"

"We saw to it that if he came to fetch Midgely he would

leave empty-handed." The King smiled at me. "Let's put it this way, Tom. Midge was already gone."

"Who took him?" I asked. "You?"

The King only smiled. I looked away, at the faint lines of ropes and masts in the fog. I couldn't see as far as the buildings, but I heard the softened rumble of the city coming awake. Lost in its crowded streets was Midgely, and I suddenly guessed who had taken him. It was someone who'd acted before the soldiers arrived to move the ship, someone whom Midgely knew and trusted, someone strong enough to lift him up the rusted old ladder. It certainly wasn't the King. I could think of only one person.

"Calliope!" I said.

The King looked astonished, perhaps amazed that I'd figured it out. "There, you see. *That's* sharp," he said. "Now let's go, Tom, and find that diamond."

I was more wary than ever. The King had lied to me more than once, and he still hadn't told me where Midgely was. Now he jumped to his feet and urged me toward the door.

Thicker by the moment, the fog swirled yellow round the ratlines. I thought I saw a movement by the rail. I definitely heard a tapping sound, a clatter in the fog.

"Someone's out there," I said.

Up from the gangway, across the deck, came Mr. Goodfellow.

It had been more than a year since I'd seen him, but he hadn't changed at all. He was *exactly* the same—in white clothes, with a white cape and a top hat. In his hand was his walking stick with its silver knob. He tapped the stick on the deck.

The little King was gawking past me. "Now who the devil's that?" he said. "Who's that fine monkey?"

I thought his eyes—older than mine—were not so strong or keen. "Why, it's Mr. Goodfellow, of course," I said.

In a flash, the King was behind the door. In another—to my great surprise—he was underneath the table. His breeches vanished last, and then he was peering out between the legs of a chair. "Is it really him? Is that what Mr. Goodfellow looks like?"

I couldn't have been more surprised. "You've never met him," I said.

"Quiet, Tom!"

"You didn't go to his office last night. Everything you've told me is a lie."

"Shhh!" said the King in a whisper. "If he finds me, he'll kill me. He's vicious, isn't he? He's mean as rats, they say."

Mr. Goodfellow, standing firmly now on the deck, adjusted his clothes. He tugged at each white glove, at each white cuff. He smoothed his side whiskers with the silver knob of his stick.

"Oh, crikey!" said the King, in a squeak. "Go and take him away, Tom. Please."

Mr. Goodfellow tapped the wood in front of him. His cape was dusted with black flecks of coal. I bent down and looked under the table, where the little King was quivering.

"Tell me the truth for once," I said. "Where's Midgely?"

"Don't ask me that."

"Where?"

"Oh, I don't know," he said. "I sent them up the ladder, among the warehouses. But, Tom—"

"Is that the truth?"

"The god's truth. I swear it." The King looked out at Mr. Goodfellow, now only yards away. "You have to save me, Tom. Please."

"Why should I save *you*?" I looked down at him, disgusted. "You schemed against me."

"It was Calliope's fault," he said desperately. "She wanted to steal the Jolly Stone from you, and . . . and the ship from Mr. Goodfellow, and . . . Oh, I tried to stop her, Tom. I tried. But you know how she is."

Mr. Goodfellow came closer. The little King, huddled into a tiny ball, begged me one more time. "Go out there and lead him away, Tom. If you save me, I'll tell you *all* the story. I can take you straight to Midgely. I swear it on my mother's grave."

But Mr. Goodfellow was already at the door. He looked in at me, and I looked out at him, and he didn't seem at all surprised to see me.

"Good day, Tom Tin," said he.

# *nineteen*

## MR. GOODFELLOW TURNS THE TABLES

Mr. Goodfellow put a hand on the top of his tall hat. He clamped it onto his head as he stooped through the door, into the cookhouse.

The last time we had been together in the same room was at the Old Bailey. He had sat high in the courtroom then, drumming his fingers on that same hat. He had drummed away while the judge delivered my sentence: transportation beyond the seas.

Though I was older and stronger now, a thrill of fear ran through me again.

"You saved my ship, Master Tin," he said. "I should thank you for that."

But he didn't.

"You've done rather well. You surprise me, in fact." That was all he said.

I could hear the King shaking. It was a rustle of clothes, a tremble of breath, like the sound of a squirrel in the forest. Mr. Goodfellow reached out and took hold of the table.

Now that table had weathered every storm in the ocean. It was a solid, heavy thing. But Mr. Goodfellow flipped it over as easily as he'd turn an egg. It crashed to the deck on its side, and there was the King in his white breeches, staring up with the most fearful look in his eyes.

"Who the devil are *you*?" said Mr. Goodfellow.

"Only a humble servant, sir," said the King. On his elbows and knees, with his round bottom in the air, he looked like a piglet on a platter.

"By what name?" said Mr. Goodfellow.

I felt pity for the little King, he trembled so badly. "George, sir," he squeaked. "George King."

"Ah," said Mr. Goodfellow. "So *you're* the wretch who married my half sister."

I was dumbfounded. There were now more sides to the story than there were facets on the Jolly Stone.

Mr. Goodfellow poked his walking stick at the little King's plump leg. "You're a fortune seeker, George. You marry your way into my business, but all you bring is ruin. No doubt you're plotting something else at this very moment."

"Oh, no, sir," said the King. "It's Tom here who's doing the plotting. I've been—"

"Do you know you've cost me a great deal of money?" said Mr. Goodfellow. He walked down the short length of the cookhouse, rapping the end of his walking stick along skillets and pans that hung on the wall. "A freed slave was found last night wandering the edge of the City. They brought someone in who spoke his lingo, and what a remarkable story the chap had to tell. I shouldn't be surprised if our loyal opposition raises some questions in the House. I'll have to grease a few palms here and there. It shall cause me a bit of bother, and not a small expense, you ham-fisted fool!"

"Mr. Goodfellow, please." The little King swiveled on his haunches to keep an eye on our visitor, who was then running his stick down a row of carving knives. "There's been a misunderstanding."

"Not at all. I understand that you're a cheat and a thief." Mr. Goodfellow put on his black hat. "You're a turncoat. That's what you are."

"Mr. Goodfellow," said George. "I had the best intentions."

"Indeed. You intended to make yourself wealthy." Mr. Goodfellow looked at me. He rapped his stick on his palm. "Master Tin, do you have the Jolly Stone?"

"Not yet," I said.

"Are you willing to find it and deliver it to me now?"

"For a price," said I.

"Well, of course there's a price. There's always a price, you young fool. I would have paid it gladly from the start," he said. "You could have saved yourself a lot of trouble, Tom. A lot of bother. Here we are, right back where we started. You have the stone, and I want it."

"But the value has increased," I said. "My price has risen."

He flushed, but managed a laugh. "Why, you *have*

learned a thing or two, haven't you? It's not the same boy who stands before me now; I see that. Perhaps there's something of your father in you after all."

This gave me a grim pleasure. For a moment I looked eye to eye with Mr. Goodfellow, and fancied that I saw something like admiration in his expression.

It was a strange moment, and the King took advantage of it by leaping from the deck. He dashed for the door.

Mr. Goodfellow whirled after him. He followed the King over the sill and out to the deck. His hat struck the top of the door and flew from his head. In the yellow fog that hung thickly now around the ship, Mr. Goodfellow raised his walking stick.

"No!" I shouted.

But down it came, and twice more. Three swift blows and a single scream, and the King lay lifeless on the deck.

"Now, Master Tin," said Mr. Goodfellow, not even out of breath. "Fetch my hat, and we'll go and get that Jolly Stone, shall we?"

It froze my blood, such a deed so easily done, so easily forgotten. I feared that I might be the next to succumb to that stick if I didn't do as I was told. Yet if I buckled under now, all would be lost.

I looked away from the crumpled body on the deck and tried to keep my voice steady. Along with the King had gone my hope of easily finding Midgely. And without Midge the Jolly Stone was that much more elusive. But I didn't let on to Mr. Goodfellow. "There are certain things I want from you," I told him.

"Mind to whom you're speaking, Master Tin," said he.

"First, you'll get pardons," I said. "For myself and the others who were with me. That's four pardons I want."

"I'm not a magistrate!" snapped Mr. Goodfellow.

"Look in your pockets," I said boldly. "Perhaps you'll find one there."

He smiled at this. "Yes, I can pull strings, Tom. Very well, you'll get your pardons. I'll have them delivered when I see the Stone."

I shook my head.

"How dare you!" said he. "I've given my word; is that not enough?"

"No, sir," I said. "It's not."

Such fury and heat came from his eyes that he might have burst into flames on the instant, consuming himself to a little heap of white ashes. But he only walked past me and got his own hat from the cookhouse floor, then led me off into the fog.

We went to his office, on the third floor of a building by the bank of the river. We walked through an enormous room packed full of clerks, all earnest young men who didn't look up from their ledgers and ink pots. The only sound came from their scribbling, as though hundreds of mice were scurrying through that cavernous space. We passed through high doorways, through rooms that were each more splendid than the last. The entire floor—the entire building, in fact—belonged to Mr. Goodfellow. There were barristers bustling about, and errand boys who went everywhere at a run, and a man whose only job was refilling the ink pots, and another who minded the lamps.

Mr. Goodfellow strode through it all, his cape flapping like wings.

A thin man fell into pace behind us, his polished shoes going *clickety-click* on the gleaming wood of the floor. He dogged us down the last corridor, through an anteroom, into Mr. Goodfellow's private office.

There I looked in wonder, all around, at a fireplace where a heap of coal glowed merrily, at a high desk so long and wide that a team of horses could have stood atop it. There were bookcases that soared to the ceiling, and chairs like the thrones of kings. I felt very tiny, and quite fragile, to be surrounded by such oversized splendor.

Mr. Goodfellow flipped off his cape, and the man was suddenly there to catch it. Then he moved behind the desk, and, quick as a wink, the man was there to pull out his chair.

"Bring your pad, Silbury," said Mr. Goodfellow, and the thin man trotted off.

The office was in a corner, with towering windows on two walls looking out on the fog and the shadows of buildings. I could hear the clang of bells and the mournful hoot of foghorns on the river, but perhaps only imagined the faint lines of masts and rigging. It was a mystery no longer how Mr. Goodfellow had known that his ship had come home. He had likely watched it sailing in.

He had to climb to a platform to sit at the desk. There, above me, he flipped through a few papers and said nothing until the thin man came clicking back to the office. Then he spoke quickly.

"Listen, Silbury. Pop round to Downing Street and see

Wellington. Give him my compliments and ask for pardons for these boys. Tom, give him the names."

I rattled them off, feeling very important that I was sending a man on an errand to see the Prime Minister of England. "And one for myself, of course," I said at the end. Silbury looked down his nose at me and said, "And *you* are?"

Mr. Goodfellow laughed. "Silbury, this is Tom Tin. The son of Redman."

"Ah," nodded Silbury. "Any news of the father? Has there been some difficulty?"

"Only that he was captured by cannibals," said I.

Mr. Goodfellow's eyes flickered with that bit of news. There seemed a hint of concern—or worry—but no more than a hint. From Silbury came a little sigh. "Ah," he said, and made a short note on his pad. I imagined he was recording the loss of a ship, or reminding himself to strike my father from the paybooks.

"Next thing," said Mr. Goodfellow. "Master Tin will be leaving with me presently. Assign him a carriage and team when he returns. We can't have him riding in a hackney, can we?" Mr. Goodfellow gave me a quick look. He may have winked; I wasn't certain. "Now, Silbury, be sure you tell Wellington this is a matter of some urgency. I need the papers on my desk by nightfall."

"Very good, sir," said Silbury.

"Have my coach brought round to the door. And send word to Doctor Kingsley that I'm on my way."

"Very good, sir." Silbury bowed, and crept from the room.

Mr. Goodfellow looked enormously pleased with himself. "You see, Tom," he said. "Even if money can't buy happiness, it certainly buys power. In my mind it buys both by the gross."

He took a cigar from a humidor made of oak and brass and mother-of-pearl. He severed its tip in a miniature guillotine that had a blade of glistening gold. Then he lit it from a gas jet that bubbled up at his touch from the top of his desk. He was soon enveloped in his own thick fog, as foul as the one outside.

"Now, Tom," he said, peering through it. "I confess that I feel rather a kinship with you. You've grown, my boy; you've changed. You're all the better for your travels, aren't you?"

I didn't answer. He still hadn't offered me a chair, and so I stood across that broad desk from him, feeling like an infant, for its top was nearly at the height of my shoulders.

"Well, you are, and you've me to thank for it. That goes without saying, though the words will never pass your lips." He sucked on the cigar, and a cloud of smoke wafted from his mouth. "What would you think if I said I might find a place for you here in the business? A junior position, mind, with Goodfellow and Company?"

I couldn't have been more surprised if he'd asked me to sit in the House of Lords. It was a flattering offer, I had to admit.

"Don't answer now," he said, raising a hand from the smoke, palm toward me. "You'll want to look before you leap, of course."

He came down from his high desk, gathered his hat and walking stick, and took me out through the building's front doors, to a busy London street. The fog restricted my view to only a few yards in either direction, so that I felt as though I looked onto a stage, where countless actors made their entrances and exits through hazy curtains. Carriages and coaches went rolling by. Hurrying businessmen, flower girls, and costermongers passed before us, all fading in and out of view.

Four snorting white horses pulled Mr. Goodfellow's wonderful carriage to the door. A footman jumped down and offered us a hand. He was wearing gloves with pearl buttons.

The coach was covered in gold leaf and gold trim. Even the rims of the wheels were polished and bright. Not a man passed without turning his head to admire it, and I couldn't help my feeling of importance as all eyes watched the footman help me up. I settled onto a seat as soft as marshmallow, looking down at a toff who was eyeing me jealously.

Mr. Goodfellow plumped himself beside me, bringing his smell of pomade and perfume. He rapped on the roof with his stick, and the mighty pull of the horses jolted me back in my seat.

He didn't ask me where the driver should go. We only started off into the fog.

# twenty

## I FIND THE STONE OF JACOB TIN

I could feel the silence in the carriage, foggy thick, as we rode along. Mr. Goodfellow, sitting very stiffly, said not a word for twenty minutes. He shined his boots on his stockings, rubbing one against the other like a big white insect. But at last he started talking.

"Calliope came to my house last night," he said. "She arrived dragging her girl—and a coffin, no less."

"It was full of toys," I said.

"Yes. I'd hoped it was full of her husband."

The city went by in the fog. Mr. Goodfellow watched through his window. "She told me about the slaves, about Beezley and the voyage home. I nearly dropped dead when she mentioned your name."

His head turned as we passed a fire-eater performing on the street. "I called straightaway for the soldiers. I went with them, down to the ship, but you'd already fled into the City."

"Did Calliope tell you—" I started. I was going to ask if he knew where Midgely was, but Mr. Goodfellow interrupted.

"She told me she was leaving that hopeless husband of hers and needed my help. Again," he said. "She had a scheme of some sort. It involved a ship—of course—and what else, I couldn't say. I wouldn't listen to a word of it, but showed her the door. The wretched woman. I put her out on her ear."

"Your own sister?"

"My *half* sister," he said.

I felt sorry for Calliope. I imagined her running from Mr. Goodfellow's home, dragging poor Charlotte as fast as she could. She must have known that Mr. Goodfellow was sending soldiers to the ship, and would have been desperate to get there before them, to snatch Midgely to safety.

"The lingering stench of a rotted marriage, that's Calliope," said Mr. Goodfellow. "The miserable product of my prodigal father's rutting with a whaler's wife." Just thinking of Calliope seemed to make Mr. Goodfellow boil with anger. "Wasteful, vulgar woman. Gallivanting across the oceans, turning up like a plague every seven years."

"I liked her," I said. It eased my mind that Midgely was safe with Calliope.

Mr. Goodfellow didn't answer. He sat grinding his hat between his hands, and it turned round and round like a black boulder in a stone mill. We traveled on through the fog.

Despite my company, and despite myself, I enjoyed that

journey. I sat at the side of the man I despised more than any other, the one I blamed for the death of my mother, the loss of my father, the ruin of my own life. Nothing but my hatred of him had kept me going through the perils of the sea, through convicts and cannibals and castaways.

Yet, somehow, it all seemed long ago and far away. There was now only this one moment of grandeur, and I let myself imagine that the carriage and the horses were mine, that I had finally attained the things I'd only dreamed of.

I sat high enough that I looked down on the crowds of people. We swept them aside as our horses cantered through the business district, our wheels spraying water from the puddles. Street sweepers bowed their heads as we passed; tradesmen touched their caps; gentlemen leapt like fleas as the water splashed on their trousers.

It occurred to me that I could do this every day if I joined Mr. Goodfellow's company. I could dash through the city and dine in the clubs. I could join the rich tide that flooded and ebbed through the doors of splendid theaters. What a flash fellow I would be! So young and so rich.

*"Do the handsome thing, my boy."* I heard the words as clearly as if my father had spoken them aloud. *"Do what's right by me, Tom,"* he'd said. Well, I was doing it! My father had spent his every penny—he'd given his all—to see that I would one day go riding through London in a fancy carriage. Oh, he'd despised the toffs himself, mocking their manners and accents, and the only swells he'd cared about were the rolling waves on the ocean. But he had wanted so badly for me to be a gentleman.

My mind suddenly leapt to the last moment I'd spent

with him. I lived it again, with every sound and smell and image. I saw the cannibals surging toward us through the shallow water, saw Father put all his strength into the last push that sent the little steamboat sliding away to safety. I heard his final words: *"Godspeed, Tom. You've done me proud, my son."* I saw the savages close around him and—

I didn't want to see any more. The pictures dissolved, leaving only the carriage window and the shapes flickering by in the fog.

A terrible emptiness followed. I found myself missing my mother with an ache that was overwhelming, longing for someone to come and tell me: What's the handsome thing to do? It was surely folly to think that Father still lived. Better to forget any hope of seeing him again, and to honor him instead. If I were rich, I could build a spectacular memorial, a tower in the middle of London, and carve his name two feet high on a tablet. Wouldn't that do him proud?

As these ideas tumbled through my mind, Mr. Goodfellow and I barreled along the streets. The carriage rocked and swayed to the surge of the horses, while a new scene appeared every moment before me. It was both grand and miserable. The fog swirled in its putrid curds, dusting the city and everything in it—from people to pigeons—with a fine coat of soot. The driver shouted; he cracked his whip. I looked out at rich and poor all squashed together, miserable beggars holding out their hands to gentlemen and ladies. Street sellers babbled about muffins and hot eels, and there was such a din of horses and crowds that I wondered if I could ever get used to it. Strange as it seemed, I missed the silence of the sea, and a fresh wind in the sails.

Mr. Goodfellow misunderstood my interest in the passing scenes. "Yes, it's all wonderful, isn't it, Tom?" he said. "No place on earth like London. You should see the Exchange, my boy; money flowing like water. Lives bought and sold. I offered to make your father a part of it, Tom; did you know that? He turned me down; said it wasn't to his liking. Well, there was never enough polish on *that* tin, if you know what I mean," he said, and he chuckled.

I didn't even smile in return, but turned my head away. We were passing through ever poorer parts of the city, so the buildings were getting smaller, the streets more narrow, as though everything was shrinking. It seemed all sad and dreary, and I thought we'd come to a part of London I had never seen. But then out from the fog slid a big wooden boot, an enormous construction hanging above a cobbler's door. I turned to watch it pass, and saw the sign of a publican that I remembered at once. Snatches of my little verses returned to my mind.

"Turn left!" I shouted.

Mr. Goodfellow nearly jumped from his seat. "Why?" he said.

"I know where the Jolly Stone is."

For a moment he gaped. Then Mr. Goodfellow banged his stick on the roof and shouted up to the driver, and I heard the horses snort as their heads were dragged around. We went clopping to the north, from street to alley. "Now turn right," I said.

For half an hour we passed along the narrow streets where Worms had driven his three-legged horse. We saw not a soul, but heard on every side the howls of cats, the barks of dogs, the colicky cries of babies. Mr. Goodfellow grew ever more excited, his voice rising in pitch as he called up directions to the driver. When we came at last to the churchyard, and I told him we'd arrived at the place where the diamond was hidden, he sounded like a little girl.

"Stop!" he cried to the driver. "Right now, do you hear? Stop!"

He fairly *hopped* from the carriage, then dragged me out behind him. "Where is it, Tom?" he said. "Where's the Jolly Stone?"

I led him round the corner and through the iron gate, in among the headstones wrapped in fog. The yellow custard was now as thick as night, the stone wall of the church a mere shadow. I felt as though I was reliving the night that I'd found and lost the Jolly Stone. I walked directly to the grave we'd opened, where my dead twin had been put to rest six feet down.

"Right here," I said, stamping my foot. "The Stone's below us."

Mr. Goodfellow went at the earth with his walking stick. He pried up the sod and the dirt. Half veiled as he was in the fog, he looked like a huge bird pecking at the graveyard grass. But his progress was slow, and his anger quick. "For heaven's sake, make yourself useful," he said. "Hurry! Go get a shovel."

"Where?" I said.

"Confound you, boy!" He bashed a tombstone with his stick. So hard did he strike it that his stick broke in two, and he whirled the handle into the fog, destroying in an instant what it would have taken my father months to earn. He cursed me. "Go tell the driver— Oh, never mind!" He cursed again. "The fellow's as much a fool as you are. I'll go with him, that's what I'll do!"

His side whiskers were shaking. "Now you stay here. Don't move from this place, do you hear me?"

With that he went storming away into the fog. I heard him swear at the driver; he even swore at the horses. There was a squeal from the springs of his carriage, the slam of a door, and the horses clomped away down the street.

It was an eerie place to be alone, a graveyard in the fog. Ravens clattered their claws on the church roof, crying out in their strange voices. Suddenly the figures on the tombstones looked more like birds of prey than angels and cherubs. For months I'd had people around me at every moment, and now I missed the closeness of the ship, the company of my friends. From there my thoughts wandered to Weedle and Boggis; were they already back on the hulks? And on to Midgely. Poor little Midge. I hoped that Calliope had taken him somewhere comfortable, that Charlotte was with him. I hated to think that he might be alone and scared.

I leapt up and paced round the graves. It was half in my mind to run from the place, and to keep running until I found Midgely. But there could be no peace for either of us without the pardons that would set us free. And for those I needed Mr. Goodfellow.

Back and forth I went among the tombstones, my eyes smarting from the yellow fog. I heard two people passing on the street, coming up to the iron gate. A woman shrieked at the sight of a ghost in the graveyard, and the footfalls hurried away.

I feared they would send a watchman, who might find me and call for the soldiers. There was probably not a Charlie brave enough to challenge spirits, but still I settled on the ground, hidden by a marble angel. I prodded at the grass, plucking worms that oozed from the gouges Mr. Goodfellow had made. Soon I found a small slab much covered with moss, and picked at it idly.

A quotation appeared: "Every man is a piece of the continent."

I took this as a wry reminder that our bodies return to the mud. Curious to see who would put a jest on his tombstone, I bared more of the tablet. Dates appeared: 1814–1827. Then the name of Jacob Tin.

I drew away from it quickly. The tablet had been shifted from its proper place, no doubt thrown aside by old Worms. It had marked the grave of the Smasher—my own twin brother—a boy I'd never known, but whose life had tangled so fully with mine.

There was a cold chill in the air now, all of a sudden. I rubbed my arms, for they'd pimpled with gooseflesh. But I couldn't look away from the stone.

The words must have been chosen by the sisters of the charity who had buried Jacob Tin, a boy of the streets. They made me understand that we were *all* tangled together. Every person I'd met in the year gone by was now entwined with every other, like so many fish scooped up in a net. From the blind man and the body snatcher, to the yellow guard at Newgate; from the farm boy on the hulk, to Mr. Mullock on his little island, they had all been drawn together, all netted from the twisting river of my fate.

I was still studying the stone when Mr. Goodfellow returned, bringing another of the familiar fish from my river. I recognized him at once as Dr. Kingsley, the buyer of corpses, for he looked no different than he had on the night old Worms had driven to his door with Jacob's white body. He had the same pointed beard, black and sharp as the ace of spades, and the same unruly hair. Now he carried a shovel, and he trod right on the stone of Jacob Tin as he jabbed the blade into the ground.

If I looked familiar, he didn't say so. He went straight to work, and we took turns digging, he and I, as Mr. Goodfellow grew ever more distraught. The hole widened and deepened, the sound of the shovel clanging through the churchyard. Dr. Kingsley wiped his brow and said, "It's like the old days, when I did everything myself. But I never thought I'd dig up an *empty* grave."

"It isn't empty, you fool," said Mr. Goodfellow. His hands were shaking. He kept looking into the fog, darting glances toward the hidden gate. "Dig, Kingsley, dig! There's a thousand guineas in each strike of the shovel."

"Why don't you sit down, Goods?" said the doctor, with quiet calm. "You'll have a stroke if you carry on like that."

Mr. Goodfellow only snatched away the shovel and pushed it into *my* hands instead. "Hurry, Tom," he said.

The ground had settled. But still I could follow the same shaft that Worms had cleared, and soon I was deeper than my own height, with a ragged square of yellow sky above me.

The shovel clinked against pebble and rock. I pushed and

pried. Then I dug in the blade, but there was no sound at all. I reached down and felt the crumbling cloth of my father's old coat.

I remembered putting it on—so long ago, it seemed. There had been pencils in the pocket, pencils that he must have sold along the streets to pay for our food and rent. Now the coat was falling away at my touch, shredding apart as though woven from cobwebs.

"I don't hear any digging," said Mr. Goodfellow.

I groped through the soil, over the rotted cloth. Twice my heart leapt to my throat when I clutched on to something hard and sharp. But both times it was only a rock, and I began to wonder if Worms hadn't kept the diamond after all. But at last I felt the huge hardness of the Jolly Stone, its edges unmistakable.

I pulled it right through the cloth of my father's coat, and saw how it glowed with the fog light. Even down there in the dark it was bright as a star. It was certainly not a doorknob; it was nothing like a doorknob. Again I could feel its heat, the burning power of all its wealth. I turned it round in my hand, marveling that I had gone so far to come back and reclaim it.

"I have it," I said.

"Pass it up, then," said Mr. Goodfellow. "Pass it up, Tom!"

I would do no such thing. I suddenly realized that I was in a very dangerous place, as the hole was too deep for me to climb out by myself. I wondered if I wasn't standing in my own grave.

# twenty-one
## MR. GOODFELLOW'S REVENGE

Mr. Goodfellow was on his knees, reaching into the grave. There were sparkles of light gleaming from his cuff links and rings. A sprinkle of dirt came down from the edge.

"The diamond, Tom! Give me the diamond," he bellowed.

I held the Jolly Stone in both hands, the riches of kings enclosed by my fingers. But I wasn't about to give up my diamond as easily as that. "You'll get it when you've kept the bargain," I said. "Not before."

"I only want to see it!" he cried, as petulant as a child. "I want to touch it. How do I know it isn't a piece of glass?"

The doctor spoke calmly, but sharply. "Look here, Goods," he said. "For the love of mercy, stop shouting at the boy. Step away, and I'll help him up."

Mr. Goodfellow's round face withdrew from the top of the hole, and in its place came the doctor's, with that devilish beard pointing right at me. "Hand me the stone, Tom," he said. "I'll hold on to it myself."

"How do I know you're not in league with him?" I asked, looking up.

Mr. Goodfellow screeched. "He's a bleeding doctor, you fool! Why do you think I dragged him along? For his health? You didn't trust *me;* I thought you might trust a bleeding *doctor*!"

"Be quiet, Goods," said the doctor, sternly. "Sit down there and don't say a word."

Another shower of dirt fell onto my shoulders. I squinted through a rain of fine dust.

"I don't blame you for being suspicious," said the doctor. "In your place I'd be the same. But if I'd come here to cheat you, don't you think I'd have done it already? Wouldn't I have clobbered you with a tombstone by now?"

Well, I could see he was right. But I dropped the Jolly Stone into my shirt before I reached for his outstretched hand. As he pulled, I scrambled to the surface, sprawling out on the grass.

"The Stone! The Stone!" said Mr. Goodfellow.

"Get ahold of yourself," snapped the doctor. "I don't want to be caught here in a graveyard, and nor do you. The boy's got the diamond; he's not running off with it."

We didn't bother to fill in the hole. We didn't even bother to fetch out the shovel. Thieves couldn't have moved any more quickly than us, and soon we were seated, all three, in Mr. Goodfellow's carriage, rumbling back toward London. I sat beside the doctor, facing forward, with Mr. Goodfellow across from us.

His knees were grass-stained, as though little green saucers had been stuck to his trousers. I, on the other hand, was smeared with dirt from head to toe. The doctor made a little joke about it. "You look like you crawled from a grave," he said, though no one laughed but he.

Mr. Goodfellow was impatient. "The diamond," he said, snapping his fingers at me. "Let's see it, Tom."

It was clear to me then that I wasn't about to be killed for the Jolly Stone. Perhaps even a snake like Mr. Goodfellow had honor inside him. Or perhaps he was happy with a thought that he was cheating me, paying a pittance for a fortune. I reached into my shirt. He leaned forward on his seat, breathing hard.

The great diamond rested cold against my stomach. But I couldn't resist pretending that I'd lost it. I groped here and there through my shirt as Mr. Goodfellow turned as white as his jacket.

"No!" he said. "No, this can't be true."

"Ho, ho!" laughed the doctor. "That's enough now, boy. You're a poor actor, and you'll give him apoplexy."

Even he fell silent when I brought out the Stone. His mouth fell open, his pointed beard stabbing at his chest. "My word!" he breathed. "Oh, my, it's fabulous."

Mr. Goodfellow was like a fat, purring cat. He actually drooled from the corners of his mouth, and his eyes were round and enormous.

In my palm the Jolly Stone glowed deep in its middle. Its hundred faces twinkled and shone. With the coach racing along, in and out of the shadows of buildings, the light played over the diamond in ever-changing ways. The Stone was now amber, now nearly purple, now red as blood through and through.

"Please let me hold it," said Mr. Goodfellow. He cupped his hands together. He reached so far, so eagerly, that he slid from his seat and came to his knees on the carriage floor. Still he held up his hands, suddenly made a beggar by his craving for the diamond.

This was the moment I'd been dreaming of and waiting for. As soon as he took the Jolly Stone he would take its curse as well. I would be freed of my worries, my bad luck outrun, and Mr. Goodfellow would begin a swift descent to ruin.

So why did I hesitate?

While I held the diamond, I was powerful and rich. I owned the wealth of kingdoms, the power to make even Mr. Goodfellow beg at my feet. But, even more, was a nagging question: Was the curse really true? Could the Jolly Stone actually wield such a force that it brought ruin to everyone who owned it?

Suddenly, the driver shouted above us. I heard the squeal of his brake, and a shift in the pattern of the horses' clattering hooves. The carriage rocked sideways and jolted to a stop.

The Jolly Stone rolled from my hand. It was like a wheel of fire leaping from my palm to my fingers, over their tips and down.

Mr. Goodfellow caught it. He snatched it to his breast and held it tight. Slowly he breathed a great breath, and lifted the Stone to his lips.

Outside, there was shouting on the streets. I could see a costermonger's cart overturned on its side, cabbages and apples spilled along the gutter. A black coach was stopped beside it, four horses in the harness. In their midst, between their hooves, lay a little girl in brown rags, and a crumpled basket of crumpled roses. There was a lot of redness on the ground, not all of it from petals.

Mr. Goodfellow had no mind for anything but the Jolly Stone. He fondled it and kissed it as a gathering crowd grew larger.

Dr. Kingsley reached across me and dropped the window open. "What's all this, then?" he said. "You, boy! What's happened?"

The boy who answered might have been any of those from the Darkey's gang. He wore a filthy jacket frayed from the cuffs to the elbows, a hat with more holes than cloth, nearly legless trousers held up with bits of string. "The toff run her over, governor," he said, touching his pathetic hat. "She didn't see him coming, she didn't."

"Wasn't she looking?" asked the doctor.

"She's blind, sir," said the boy. He pointed to the curb. "She was with that costermonger, sir."

I saw a small, burly man at the side of the road. He was trying to guard his poor cabbages, shouting at the children—the men and women—who were trying to pilfer them. He scurried back and forth, snatching them up. But they tumbled from his arms as quickly as he collected them.

"That's her father," said the boy.

The carriage had thrown a wheel. Even as the flower girl

lay between the horses, men were trying to jack it up, to fit a new wheel on the hub. A man still sat inside, staring bleakly from a window.

Dr. Kingsley opened his door.

"Where do you think you're going?" said Mr. Goodfellow.

"To help that girl," said he.

Mr. Goodfellow took his first look through the window. All he said was, "What a bother!"

We didn't wait for the doctor. Mr. Goodfellow hammered at the roof, and the driver worked our carriage through the crowd. People moved aside to let us by, and the last I saw was Dr. Kingsley stooping down between the horses.

We coached directly to Mr. Goodfellow's office. He never let go of the diamond, and I never asked him to. He carried it up to the third floor, down the row of clerks. He shouted, "Silbury!" Then he climbed up behind his desk, opened a drawer, and locked the Jolly Stone inside it.

Silbury came into the office. He glanced at me, but spoke to Mr. Goodfellow. "The pardons have arrived, sir. They're in that yellow folder on your—"

"Yes, yes. Very well," said Mr. Goodfellow. "Go down and find Mr. Roberts, will you?"

"Mr. Roberts, sir?"

"Have you gone deaf, Silbury? Find him and bring him here."

"Yes, sir."

I walked up to the desk, feeling ridiculously small behind it. "I've decided," I said, "that I don't want to join your company."

Mr. Goodfellow raised his eyebrows. "Oh, you don't?"

"No, sir," I said. "I don't want any of the things you offered me. I don't want to be a gentleman."

It seemed he couldn't look in my eyes. He kept watching the door instead. "Well, what *do* you want, Tom? The Jolly Stone, I suppose; is that it?"

"No. The ship," said I. "Give me the ship that I brought to the Pool. In exchange for the diamond, give me the ship."

He stared at me for a moment, then answered with one short word. "Done."

"And provisions for a voyage."

"Done," he said.

"And a captain and crew paid off for two years."

"Done. What else?"

"That's all," I said.

"It's nothing." He drew a pad toward himself and scribbled a few lines. With that—a bit of ink and an instant of his time—he gave me all that I wished, and it seemed like untold riches to me. I didn't want to live in a place where a blind girl was of less importance than a carriage wheel, of less value than cabbages. I couldn't wait to be away from London, away from the fog and the crowds and the people like Mr. Goodfellow. I would go back to the southern seas and search for my father. I would "do him proud," in the way that he must really have hoped that I would.

Mr. Goodfellow slid the paper toward me. He did it slowly, as though he had second thoughts about the whole business. I could hear Silbury coming back through the halls, now with a second set of shoes tapping along with his.

"Well, Tom," said Mr. Goodfellow. "A year ago I would

have signed over the ship, and taken the diamond, and that would have been the end of it. But now . . ." He spread his hands apart. "Well, I confess to a worry about this. You've grown wiser and stronger, and one day you might come back and claim the Jolly Stone. You might say you weren't fully paid, or that I cheated it from you."

"I won't do that," I said. "You have my word."

He laughed. "Your *word*! You wouldn't take mine, would you? Well, my boy, I trust no one. Especially a Tin."

The footfalls were louder, the men very close. Mr. Goodfellow wore his look of smug pleasure. "You're already like your father," he said. "You'll come to the same miserable end, I'm sure. Do you know he stood where you're standing now, a pigeon waiting for crumbs to be tossed in his direction?"

"My father never begged from you, and nor will I." We glared at each other across that huge desk. "Give me the paper, Mr. Goodfellow, if you have any honor left at all."

Silbury and his companion entered the office, their footfalls suddenly stopping. Mr. Goodfellow put his fat palm on the paper and drew it back toward himself. In a voice that was deep and loud he said, "Mr. Roberts!"

The man answered from behind me. "Yes, sir. Here, sir."

I turned to see a very hairy fellow in a very shiny uniform. He must have fancied himself as a king's guard, judging by all the gold tape he'd sewn to his clothes. He looked like a drum major, but he was no more than a policeman of sorts.

"Look at this boy!" intoned Mr. Goodfellow. "He's trying to rob me!"

"Wh-what?" I stammered.

"Furthermore," said Mr. Goodfellow, "the boy's a convict. He escaped from a transport ship."

I tried to argue, but it was no use. Who would have taken the word of a boy stained head to toe from robbing graves? Mr. Roberts pulled a rope from his waist, and in a moment he had twisted it round my wrists, and my hands behind my back.

"Get him out of my sight," said Mr. Goodfellow. "Take the cockroach away."

# twenty-two
## MY PROMISE TO WEEDLE

What happened next is too hard to be told in detail. I spent a miserable night in a London jail, and late the next day I was driven through the fog, over the river and east toward Chatham.

The driver chose London Bridge as his route across the Thames. I looked down on the Pool and saw the ship—*my* ship—faint and blurred in the fog. I saw the stairs where Calliope must have dragged poor Midgely up to the City, and thought of my little friend waiting for me. I wondered if he had already decided that I must have forsaken him.

We made no stops except those necessary for the horses. But the roads were rough, the coach was slow. The sun was near to setting when we arrived at the Medway and I looked out again on the horrible hulk *Lachesis*. It sat chained in place, fettered to the river bottom, as black and bleak as ever.

From that first glimpse, I couldn't take my eyes from the ship. With its masts cut to stumps, its round hull high in the water, it looked unbelievably ugly, as evil as a thing could be. It rumbled with the clank of chains as four hundred boys, all dragging their irons, tramped to their dinner. It oozed a clammy sadness clear across the river.

A boat waited at the shore to ferry me there. As I stepped into it I thought how the next time my feet touched land it would be on Australian soil.

The boatman didn't speak to me. I sat with my lip quivering, but determined not to cry. The hulk seemed to grow bigger and darker as we rowed toward it. I heard the steady thump and spurt of water pumping from the hull, the gurgle of the river flowing past the hulk.

The oarsman misjudged the speed of the currents. We banged against the ship, then grated down its long side. There was a band of mussels and weeds and withered sponges above the water, bared by the pumping that had lightened the ship. We scraped it away with our bow, peeling off the mussels, curling the weeds, until we came to a heavy stop at the landing.

I climbed to the deck, nearly wishing I were climbing a gallows instead. Men dragged me to the pump, where I was washed naked in the icy spray of a hose. I was given the canvas shirt and trousers that I would wear all the way to Botany Bay. Then the Overseer himself came with my hammock, and he remembered me at once.

"Ah, the boy who escaped from my chapel," he said.

"You'll not repeat that trick, I promise you. Ten days from now you'll be on your way again to Australia." He had the blacksmith fit me with doubled irons. Then he clouted my ears for good measure and sent me below to the darkest and deepest part of the hulk.

The boys were at service, the hammocks yet to be hung. I went straight to the window; it was heavily barred. There I stood, gazing out on the river and the hills and the fleet of ships at the bend, all fading to purple in the sunset. I could see the nob of Beacon Hill above the village where I was born.

I worked my hand between the bars, stretching as far as I could, until my shoulder was jammed against them. My arm scraped on mussels and barnacles, but I reached farther—as far as I could—and dabbled the very tips of my fingers in the Medway. I wanted to taste again the blood of England, as though it might give me strength.

I heard the faint chime of the ship's bell marking the half hour. That sound was worse than the clanking of irons, worse than the shouts of the guards. It was the sound that would never stop, that would come twice an hour through every hour of every day. It tolled for all the time before me, seven years of hulks and ships and prison camps. I heard it, and I cried for myself in that place. How could I have let Mr. Goodfellow lead me along? I had given up a diamond that couldn't have been cursed at all.

I kept seeing his face—in the ripples of the river, on the moon that sailed above the hills. I heard his voice. *"What a bother!"*

I was still at the window when the bell rang again, and

the boys came back from chapel. I heard the tramp of their feet, the rumble of their chains, but I didn't turn around. I knew the nobs would come straight to me, and they did. There were five or six of them, and they stood at my sides and my back, crowding me against the curved side of the ship. They plucked at my clothes and pulled at my hammock. "What's your name, nosey?" they asked. "What you done, nosey?"

I had seen what nobs would do to a boy who didn't fight back. I had seen arms broken and eyes punctured. I had seen boys starved to skeletons as each of their meals was stolen away. But I didn't turn from the window. I couldn't let them see that my eyes were red, that my cheeks were wet with tears.

"The nosey ain't talkin'," said one of the nobs. Another pushed me, so that my shoulder banged against the wood.

I knew I could call for a guard. There was a slim chance that one might even come if I did. He could save me then, but not later that night. When the ship was locked down, the guards deserted the lowest deck, and the nobs had the run of the ship.

Again I was pushed into the window. Next would be the punches, the fists and the feet.

"Leave me alone," I said. "All of you leave me alone."

"What if we don't?" they said, and laughed. "What are you going to do, nosey?"

My tears ran right into my mouth, their taste more salty than the river. But as the nobs jostled, a rage began to grow inside me. It pushed away my sadness and my fears, until it filled me from head to toe. It was the same blinding anger that had come before, when I'd been pushed too far by others. It was that dark, scary part of my soul that belonged to the Smasher, my dead twin.

The nobs taunted me. They pushed harder. More of the boys began to gather around, eager to see a beating or, better, a real fight.

I let the hammock fall at my feet. I pumped my hands into fists.

"Come on, nosey," said one of the nobs. His cry was taken up by others. Then I recognized among the squabble the voice of Walter Weedle. To my surprise he wasn't urging the others on, but trying to hold them back.

"Wait! Do you know who that is?" he said. "That's the Smasher, he is."

As though he'd fired a shot at circling wolves, the boys drew back. One of them said, "The Smasher's dead." Another said, "His grave was opened; that's what I heard. He come out of his grave, the Smasher did." There was much muttering, and another clear voice. "No, that can't be the Smasher."

"Take a look!" cried Weedle. He grabbed my shoulder, and in one move he turned me round and bared my arm, showing the diamond-shaped scar where my father had cut me apart from Jacob.

The nobs stepped back. A space opened between us, and only Weedle stayed beside me. "See, it's him, ain't it?" he said. "Sure as spit it's him."

I looked back into the faces of the nobs. I didn't fear them, and they must have seen that. If there were still runnels of tears on my face, it didn't matter. There wasn't one of those nobs who hadn't wept into a hammock at night, muffling sobs with his hands. They were only boys, after all.

The ship's bell rang above us. The convicts began to form into lines, ready to shuffle up to the deck where the hammocks were stored. Some of the nobs moved eagerly away at the chance, while others lingered as long as they could.

Weedle was the only one who didn't wander off. He shouted a strange name at a boy. "You. Lumps! Bring my hammock for me."

The lines of convict boys went marching off, dragging chains down the long groove in the deck. Weedle watched them go.

"You was going to fight them, weren't you, Tom?" he said. "You was going to fight them all."

I shrugged. The rage had left me then, and I was feeling rather shaky. "Thank you for saving me," I said.

"Well, you saved me on them islands," he said rather grandly. Then he frowned and squirmed. "Here, will you promise me something, Tom? I'm king of the nobs again, Tom. Swear you won't tell them I was smugging snow."

I nearly laughed. I'd forgotten that Weedle was on the hulks only because he'd stolen the "snow" of ladies' white petticoats. I said I would never tell a soul.

He smiled at me, satisfied. "Tom, who sent the soldiers to the ship?" he asked.

"Mr. Goodfellow," I said.

"That toff in the white coat? He came with the soldiers, Tom. More soldiers than I ever seen. They took Gaskin too."

"Where is he?" I asked.

Weedle pointed upward with his thumb. For a horrible moment I thought he meant that Boggis had died and gone to heaven. But he told me that the guards had put Boggis on an upper deck, where the ceiling was higher.

"So we're all here but Midgely," he said. "Might turn out he's the lucky one, being blind and all. Better he's gone to his Maker without ever seeing the hulks again."

"Don't talk like that. He isn't *dead,*" I told Weedle. "I don't know where he is, but he's safe. Calliope will look after him."

"How could Calliope find him?"

"Why, she's the one who took him away," I said. "You must have been there when it happened. It was before the soldiers got to the ship."

*"Calliope?"* Weedle looked puzzled. "Why didn't she save me and Gaskin then, Tom? And why was Midgely screaming? We was up in the bow, looking at the lights in the City, when we heard him shouting for help."

"Are you sure?"

"Yes, Tom. He screamed and cried and shouted your name. That was the last we heard, him shouting for you, Tom. Whoever it was, they went right up that old ladder. Gaskin was going to go after him, but the soldiers came right then."

I sank to my knees on the deck. The thought of blind Midge being dragged away was bad enough; what had happened to make him so afraid of Calliope? But that he went shouting my name was worse. He must have felt betrayed and abandoned. I remembered the bitter words of our parting, and wished I could take them back.

Weedle stood awkwardly beside me until the boys came

down with the hammocks. As king of the nobs, he had the place nearest to the window, and he saw to it that my hammock was hung beside his. Then, in our irons we climbed aboard them, and the ship was locked down for the night. In the darkness, amid the clinking of chains and the sobbing of boys, Weedle reached out and touched my arm.

"Don't think about it, Tom," he said.

"I had pardons," I told him. "That's the worst of it. I had pardons for us all, but they'll never be delivered now."

Weedle lay for a few moments in silence. Then his head poked up from his hammock, his long scar standing out in a white streak, the way it always did when he was alarmed. "Tom, I don't want no pardon," he said. "I'm a proper nob now. If they send me to Australia I'll be a holy terror there. I think I was meant to be a nob, Tom, like you was meant to be a sailor. Promise you'll stop my pardon if you can."

That Weedle thought of me now as a sailor was a small comfort in my misery. I agreed to his request, then lay on my back with the ceiling just inches above me. Before the moon had set, the nobs would go roving through the ship. The cries of the noseys would ring out from here and there, but I would be left alone. I was the Smasher. I had gone into his grave, and come out from his grave, and finally taken his place.

I thought I would be the Smasher forevermore, that this would be the end of my tale. But only six days I spent on the hulk. On the seventh morning I went to my grave again.

## *twenty-three*
## THE DAY OF MY DEATH

My sixth day on *Lachesis* began like all the others. I carried my hammock up to the deck, went down to my breakfast, and then to my work. I sewed together two pieces of cloth, over and over, again and again.

At noon I took my "stroll" along the deck, shuffling along in my place in the line, trying to hold my chains so that the shackles wouldn't scrape the skin from my ankles. I could see Boggis trudging along ahead of me, some fifty boys between us. I had seen him then a few times, and was no longer shocked by his sad and shrunken appearance.

I ate my meals, went to chapel, fetched my hammock back. I did it all to the clear strokes of the ship's bell, wishing I could tear the thing from its mount and hurl it to the river.

The sixth night began clear and starry. Through the window came reflections from the water, rippling on the ceiling above me as I lay in my hammock. The ropes that held it, like the ropes that held the countless others, creaked in their iron hooks. The boys coughed and sobbed, and their chains rattled.

From a deck above me I heard one of the convicts cry out. This had happened every night at the same time, the same boy crying the same words. "No, don't!" he shouted in the most heart-wrenching tones. "No! Please don't!"

I didn't know what was happening to the boy who lay shrieking. I didn't *want* to know that. It was bad enough I knew the voice. It was Gaskin Boggis. On his own deck, a group of nobs every night went at him.

"He fought back the first night," said Weedle, beside me. "But the guards put him in the black hole, so he stopped."

Boggis had seen the wide world. He was like Oten Acres and all the farm boys who—without their huge horizons—were always the first to waste away in the hulk. Without hope for a pardon, he wouldn't have long for the world.

On this sixth night, like all the others, I lay rigid in my hammock, squeezing my fists so tightly that I tore the skin on my palms. "Please, stop! Leave me alone." Gaskin's cries went on for half an hour, between the chimings of the bell, until the heavy footfalls of a guard brought silence to the deck.

I turned my face toward the window and lay for a while staring out. All I could see was the water, the small waves painted silver by the starlight. I could hear them lapping against the wooden side of the hulk.

The guard came down. He carried his lantern along the deck, then up the next set of stairs. As soon as he'd gone I rolled out of my hammock and went to the window.

I pushed my arm through a gap in the bars. Already it was easier to do. The prison food—so sparse, so awful—had left me weak and hungry. But at least I could reach farther through the bars.

I picked two mussels. Every night I picked two mussels. I pulled them from that band of dried weeds and barnacles, and brought them in through the window.

They had been out of the water long enough now that they were half dead and easy to open. From the shells I scraped the lumps of orange flesh, and tried to lick away what juices were left. Then I carried my little treasures back to my hammock.

As always, I offered one of the bits of meat to Weedle. He wasn't as hungry as I was since, as a nob, he took a share of each meal from the smaller boys. But still he never got enough, and I could see he was tempted to share the mussels when I held out my hand to his hammock.

"Go on," I said. "Take one."

"Not me. They ain't no good, Tom," he said. "One night you'll get a bad one, you'll see."

I always laughed at his fears. But that night he was right.

I swallowed the mussels whole, one after the other. It was like swallowing gobs of spit. They were horrible things, but they kept my stomach busy.

It was only a few moments later that my lips began to tingle. Then my stomach seemed to twist itself into a knot. I groaned.

"You see? You see?" said Walter Weedle. "Didn't I tell you, Tom?"

The tingling spread to my lips, then leapt to my fingertips. I felt incredibly hot, as though my skin were melting, but when I touched my face I found I couldn't feel it. My fingers had gone numb.

I suddenly wanted water. I was desperately thirsty. I tried to swing out of my hammock but tumbled from it instead, crashing to the deck.

"Tom, what are you doing?" said Weedle. "You'll bring the guards."

I hobbled to the window. I thrust my arm through the bars and reached down as far as possible. I couldn't tell if I touched the water until I raised my hand and saw my fingers glistening with wetness. I sucked the salty dew and reached for more.

Now the hulk seemed to pitch as though in a storm. I clung to the window so that I wouldn't be thrown across the deck. Then the sight of the hammocks hanging perfectly still sent a wave of fear right through me. I let go of the window bars and put my hands to my face. I reeled away from the wall and collapsed on the deck.

"Tom?" said Weedle. "Tom!"

He came to my side. All around, white faces popped out from the edges of hammocks.

Weedle shook me. He shook me so hard that he rattled my teeth together and banged my head on the deck. "What's wrong? What's wrong?" he shouted.

I tried to tell him what was happening, but my lips and mouth were now so numb that they wouldn't form the words.

Then I found with horror that I couldn't lift an arm to save myself. From head to toe, through and through, I was powerless to move a muscle.

I could draw only the smallest breaths. My heart, which had been racing desperately, seemed to stop altogether. There was only a mere tremble of blood through my veins.

Yet I could hear and see and understand all that was happening. Boys began to mutter, then to shout. A guard came running with his lantern.

Weedle slapped my cheeks to bring life to them. It was the most curious, frightening thing to hear the slaps of his fingers, but not to feel the blows. He took me again by the shoulders, trying to shake me awake.

That was how the guard found him, kneeling over my chest as though he had beaten me to death. The guard whistled for others, then bashed at Weedle with his stick. A hundred boys came hurtling from their hammocks, and I lay surrounded by pandemonium, certain that I was about to die.

When what had happened was all sorted out, and the guards stood heaving breaths at one side of the hulk, the boys at the other, the doctor at last came down. He bent over me.

I couldn't even move my eyes. I could see only what was straight ahead. The doctor's face loomed over me, and then Weedle's as he peered anxiously over the doctor's shoulder.

"It was them mussels," said Weedle. "I tried to tell him they was no good." He was bleeding from his nose. There was a red welt on his cheek, and the red marks of fingers on his neck. "Is he going to die, doctor?"

"I'm afraid he already has." The doctor put his hand on my chest.

I couldn't feel it, though I sensed he was pressing very hard. I tried to talk, but that was impossible. I couldn't even push the air through my mouth.

"Yes, he's cold as ice," said the doctor. "No trace of a heartbeat. He's gone already."

*No! No!* I shouted in my mind. But there was not a sound from my lips, not a quiver from my tongue.

"He's dead?" said Weedle, unbelieving.

"As doornails," said the doctor.

"No, it can't be. He saved us from the cannibals. He brought us home, he did. It just can't be."

"Well, it is," said the doctor, rising to his feet. "Guards, carry him up to the deck."

One took my shoulders, another my legs, and they bore me like a sack of rubbish up the many stairs. I watched the roof beams pass above me, then the square of stars in the hatch turning round and round as we rose toward them. They dropped me onto the deck, in the open air, by the gate in the railing where steps went down to the river.

The blacksmith came and took away my irons. Then another man brought a strip of canvas and bundled me inside it. I saw his needle passing in and out of the cloth as he sewed me into my shroud.

How long I lay there I don't know. It seemed an eternity before I was carried down to a boat and placed awkwardly between the thwarts. I could hear two men talking, and a third rowing. He used short and choppy strokes that splashed water onto one of the other fellows.

I had fought with cannibals. I had nearly drowned in storms at sea. I had faced strange beasts, and stranger men, but I had never been more terrified than I was in that boat, sewn into my shroud. With my every muscle paralyzed, and my brain whirling from the horror, I went toward my end without the slightest hope of escaping. I tried to kick my legs and thrash my arms; in my mind I was doing just that. But I couldn't move enough to put even a ripple in the canvas.

"Poor lad," said one of the men. "Wasn't on the hulk a week, you know. A few more days, he'd be off to Australia."

The other spat. "Well, he's off just the same, ain't he? Going down under. Only not the way he thought he would."

"It's for the better, I suppose. The lad probably never had two pennies to knock together, and never the hope he would. Better he go to his rest now, and save himself the suffering."

They fell silent then, probably turning their heads to watch the sunrise. I could see the light through the canvas, the cloth turning brown.

"Rain this morning," said one of the men.

It wasn't long before I heard the boat grind up onto the riverbank, and the men splash ashore. I was heaved out as rudely as I'd been heaved in, and half dragged through the mud. Again I was set down, as the shoveling began.

One of the men must have been the chaplain. I heard him praying over me, asking God to accept my soul. Then he pressed something to my chest—a crucifix, perhaps. I saw the cloth pucker round it, and his shadow fall across the canvas.

I felt the touch of his hand!

Where before I had no feeling, I could now sense the pressure of his fingers. The poison was surely passing through me, fading from my flesh.

But too late. I was picked up and tossed down. I only vaguely felt the jarring thump as I landed in my grave. I heard the shovel pushing into dirt, then the pattering hail of the first clods falling onto my shroud. I began to feel their weight as they piled heavily on my feet, on my shins and my knees.

Desperately, I tried to move, to signal that I was still alive. The dirt kept falling by the shovelful.

I could feel the coarse canvas pressing at my elbows and hips. I was aware of my heart quickening. But still I was unable to move as the clods of dirt fell upon me. They covered my chest, then pattered down onto my head. I could feel each and every one.

I put my whole mind to making a sound. I forced air in and out of my lungs. I believed I was roaring, but it must have been no more than a whisper.

Then the shoveling stopped. "Did you hear that?" said one of the men.

Again I roared.

"There!" cried the fellow.

"Don't be daft. I can't hear a thing," said the other.

"He's whispering, he is. He's whispering, I tell you!"

With a flash of hope I thought the men would clear away the dirt and haul me from the ground. But all they did was run away. "He's covered enough," said the first fellow. "The rain will do the rest."

I heard them bolt across the marsh. The grasses slithered, and birds cried out. The thump of the oars came soon after, and I lay in the ground all alone.

The rain began as a soft drizzle on the canvas. Then it fell more heavily, until it beat at the ground with a hiss and a rush, likes waves out on the ocean. My grave slowly filled with water, and its sides collapsed around me, so that it seemed I would drown in the earth.

# twenty-four
## THE BONE GRUBBER'S FRIGHT

What a sad and terrible end it seemed I had come to. The ground softened into mud that oozed all around me, welling over my chest, covering my chin. It cast a mold of my body, as though I were an insect encased forever in amber.

If, in a hundred years—or a thousand years—someone happened to come across my grave, he would think I'd been laid peacefully to my rest. He would see no sign of the horror I'd felt as the mud rose up to choke me. He would never guess I'd been buried alive.

As the canvas soaked with rain, and the melting mud was painted across it, my darkness deepened. It made me think of Midgely, and how brave he was to have never complained. The thought of that brought something of a calm over me.

I lay and waited—I could do nothing more nor less—listening to the rain and the push of waves against the riverbank. I began to understand how Midge had come to "see" with his ears, in a manner of speaking. I could tell the river was rising, and knew when it advanced as far as the grasses. I heard it creep closer, and imagined the mice and the shrews retreating before it.

Next I heard a squash of mud, a creak of wood. I "saw" the grasses bend and crush below the turning wheel of a wagon. I "saw" the mud squirting up around the horse's hooves. There was a strange pattern in the animal's steps, but it puzzled me for only a moment.

With a clarity that would have startled Midgely, I "saw" the horse in every detail. I saw it with three legs and a wooden stump, with a straw hat slit for its ears, in a glistening coat of leather and cloth and metal scraps. I saw the driver in his greasy clothes, in his hood and hat and gloves, swaying on the seat as the wagon tipped its way across the dunes. But of course I knew them well, old Worms and his three-legged horse.

I heard him call, "Whoa, Peggy!" then clamber down to the mud. I heard him work the latch at the back of the wagon and open the drawer that hid his gruesome cargo.

There was a trudging in the mud, the sound growing louder. Soon came a laugh. "Hookey Walker!" shouted Worms. "Here's one what don't even need digging, Peggy. He's come up to the surface like a grub."

I knew then that I was safe. Worms hauled me from the ground and carried me away on his shoulder. I could feel his hands holding me, and smell all the stinks that came from his bone grubber's clothes. He rolled me off onto the hard planks of the wooden drawer, then slit my shroud with a knife. The blade nearly cut through my nose; it nearly stabbed my eye. Then his fingers came through the gap and pulled the cloth aside, and I was looking right into his face.

I saw it all at once: his grimy hat and black hood; the look of sad surprise that came over him.

"By jabers!" he said. "It's that boy from London, Peggy. Tom Tin; that were his name. Wal-ker! I thought he'd amount to something, that one. Not come to his end in a convict's grave. He must have gone back on the tidy dodge."

I put all my strength and all my will into moving my muscles then. It took every ounce of effort to manage so much as a wink. But I did it! I winked one eye at the body snatcher, and he leapt back as though I'd taken him by the throat.

"Hookey Walker!" he cried again. "Lord have mercy, he's alive!"

Worms bent over me. He patted my cheeks; he nipped them in his fingers. "I've got just the ticket," he said, and fetched from his wagon a little brown bottle that he put to my lips.

It was tonic and whisky and pine tar and rum. But mostly it was whisky, and it burned my tongue and clogged my throat; I hadn't the strength to swallow.

He tipped up my head and emptied the bottle into my mouth. It was the searing shock of it that must have brought me to my senses, for I coughed and wretched, and suddenly my lungs were filling with air. I couldn't move my arms or legs, but my fingers were twitching of their own accord.

"There, you're back. You're back," said Worms. "Oh, mercy, Tom Tin, you gave me half a fright, you did."

My head lolled to one side. I could see across the marshes and out to the river, all gray and gloomy in the rain. The hulk of *Lachesis* was no more than a looming shape, but I feared that someone there was watching this all.

"Please," I managed. "Take me away."

Worms had the same fear of being spotted. He pushed me down into the drawer. "Best you stay out of sight till we're clear of the marshes," he said. Then he slid me into the wagon, took his seat, and drove off.

And so I began my trip toward London, lying in the very same place where my twin had lain when Worms had dragged *him* from his grave. At first I bounced and tumbled with the wagon's motion, but the feeling returned to my arms, and I was able to brace myself as we rolled out from the dunes to the road.

A mile or two on our way, Worms stopped and let me out. He added my burial shroud to his box full of rags, and dressed me in clothes that he'd gathered from dustbins. When I sat up beside him, I looked every inch a grubber.

He carried me straight into London, and what a pleasure it was—despite the stench of the rancid fat and dog droppings that he'd gathered—to ride the body snatcher's wagon instead of Mr. Goodfellow's elegant carriage. Worms listened to the story of my adventures, adding excited exclamations of "Fancy that!" or "Mercy me!" When he'd heard the end of it he insisted on taking me right where I wanted to go—right to the door of Mr. Goodfellow's building.

"I'll come up if you like, Tom," he said, as he drew the wagon to a stop. "Fancy toffs like him, they don't give me no fears. I wouldn't lift me hat to none of them."

I thanked him, but refused. "I have to go myself," I said.

"'Course you do."

When I stood on the street below him, Worms looked down and smiled. "You've made me happy, Tom Tin," he said. "When I seen you in that shroud I thought you'd come to a bad end. But you've turned from a boy to a man, I see, and it's all from me kindness, ain't it? It's from that leg up I gave you."

I had nearly forgotten that he had put two pennies in my hand long ago, to start me on my way. I *did* remember that I'd laughed at him, behind his back, because he was so poor and filthy while I owned the wealth of the Jolly Stone. I'd imagined telling my rich friends how a bone grubber had given me food. Now I regretted that very much. I would rather spend the rest of my days with the likes of Worms than with men like Mr. Goodfellow.

He tipped his hat to me. "God bless you, Tom Tin," he said, and clucked softly at Peggy. I watched him rumble away, into the twisting lanes of old London. Then I gathered myself to face Mr. Goodfellow.

I marched up the stairs and through his office. The clerks looked up from their ledgers, aghast at the sight of a boy in rags in a place as fine as that. Silbury came sweeping out from some dark corner and fell in beside me.

"What do you think you're doing, boy?" he said. "Where are you off to?" His shoes twinkled as he scampered along. "Answer me, blast you!"

I stopped. He trotted past, then turned about. "Oh, it's you," he said. "It's Tom Tin."

"I've come to see Mr. Goodfellow," said I.

"Well, you can't." He held up a small hand, so clean that it shone. "He's not seeing anyone, boy. He hasn't moved from his office in three days."

"Then I'll have no trouble finding him, will I?" With a push I was past. Silbury fell aside, and a gasp came up from the clerks.

"Stop!" he cried. "If you don't, I shall call for Mr. Roberts."

"Start calling," I said without slowing.

He shouted the name through the halls as I strode along. I came to the doors of Mr. Goodfellow's office, turned the handle, and threw them open. They banged against the walls with a blow that set the gas lamps fluttering.

Mr. Goodfellow was not at his high desk. He was seated instead in a three-wheeled chair that someone had pushed to the windows to give him a view. His back was toward me, but in a fashion that was almost pathetic to see, he shifted the chair until he faced me.

A red blanket was drawn over his knees and his lap, and in the middle of it lay the Jolly Stone.

He had aged a year in the week gone by. His face was haggard and drawn, his hair all limp and gray. There was a smell of sweat about him instead of perfume, and one of his hands had a tremor in it.

"I saw you coming," he said, cradling the Stone in his fingers. "A bone grubber's wagon, no less. My, wouldn't your father be proud? I believe you've outdone him, my boy."

The window toward the river was open, letting in the sounds of ships and sailors. The air, not yet tainted by fog, gave to the curtains the same tremble of Mr. Goodfellow's hand. I could have gone to the chair and tipped him out of it, through his window and down to the street. But I saw that the diamond was already working its evil, and I liked that his end would come more slowly.

"Damn your eyes, Tom Tin," he said. "The Stone has a curse in it, doesn't it?"

"So it seems," I said.

He looked down at the Jolly Stone. The colors flashed up from it, glinting in his eyes. "I've lost two thousand guineas already. Three hundred a day since it came to my hands. It robs wealth, doesn't it? That's the curse of the thing."

He laughed a hollow laugh. "Well, thank God it robs years as well; I shan't die penniless, Tom. I'll still have more money than *you'll* ever see."

I climbed up to his desk. The pardons were laid upon it, along with the note that gave me his ship. They were weighed down by a money purse made of silk from the Orient.

"Take them, Tom," said Mr. Goodfellow. "And the wretched ship as well. I've thirty other ships, you know; the one means nothing to me. You'll find it in Limehouse Reach, provisioned and ready for sea."

I looked toward the door, expecting Mr. Roberts to appear any moment.

"Don't worry; there's no trick," said Mr. Goodfellow. "I'm giving you your freedom, Tom. For the rest of your life you'll be in my debt."

"I owe nothing to you," said I. "You *stole* my freedom, Mr. Goodfellow. You don't give it to me; you only return it."

"You ungrateful little swine." He turned the diamond in his hands, round and round like a ball of flames. "Who do you think propped you up all your life, Tom? It was I who kept your father solvent, so that you might cling to your mother's apron strings. Well, you'll have to stand on your own feet now, my boy, and you'll find the world hard enough. That ship will be your prison, and one day your scaffold too, I'm sure. You were never meant to amount to much, Tom Tin."

He delivered these words with great bitterness, and they made me flush through and through. So he had never believed I'd bettered myself. He had never wanted me in his business.

"Where can I find Calliope?" I asked.

"I've no idea," said he. "Nor do I care."

"Do you know where Midgely is?"

"I don't even know *what* a Midgely is." Mr. Goodfellow coughed horribly, then spat into a handkerchief. "Curse you, Tom. I'm dying already."

I put the papers in my shirt. I stepped down from the desk and walked in front of it just as Mr. Roberts came rushing into the office in his glittering uniform.

# *twenty-five*

## WHAT BECAME OF MR. GOODFELLOW

Mr. Goodfellow shouted from his chair. "Get out!" he cried. His voice, once fierce, had a quaver in it. "If I want you, Mr. Roberts, I shall call for you," he said.

"But, sir, the boy's a convict. Silbury said—"

"Silbury's a fool." Mr. Goodfellow could still manage a glare that would melt stone. "The boy has a pardon—from Wellington, no less. Now get out and leave us alone."

Mr. Roberts backed out of the office. I took one more look at Mr. Goodfellow in his chair, then turned to leave as well. I was halfway to the door when he called my name.

"Tom, wait," he said.

I turned back.

He had his eyes cast down. His trembling fingers sent

ripples through the red blanket. "I keep thinking of camels and the eyes of needles," he said quietly. "Tom, I'm scared of dying."

I came as close as I ever could to feeling pity for the man. He looked old and weak and sad.

"If you want me to beg, Tom, I will," he said. "Tell me; is there any way to rid myself of the curse?"

I wanted to tell him that there wasn't. But I saw him shivering below his blanket, feeling the cold from the open window and the gathering fog. Yellow tendrils were tangling now round the tallest buildings, round the dome of St. Paul's and the lofty monument to the fire.

"There *is* a way, isn't there?" he said. "I see how you hesitate, Tom. Please, if you've learned an ounce of benevolence, tell me. How do I destroy the curse?"

I had to smile to myself, and not for any gloating over the withered man before me. Benevolence was exactly what I'd learned in my travels. Gone was the selfish, coddled boy, and in his place was one who truly cared for the welfare of others. Strange as it seemed, it was all because of Mr. Goodfellow's mean spirit.

"Tell me, tell me!" He reached up his grayed hands, the wonderful Jolly Stone shining between them. "How do I rid myself of the curse?"

"By ridding yourself of the diamond," I said.

"Is there no other way?"

I only shook my head. I watched him cradle the Stone to his breast like a baby, and turned again to leave him. But in the doorway I heard the creak of his chair, and the soft thump of his blanket falling to the floor. I looked back to see him standing unsteadily at the window, his arm cocked back, the Jolly Stone in his fist, about to be hurled out to the river.

"No!" I shouted.

He threw the Stone as far as he could. It went up in an arc through the window. For an instant I saw it suspended above all the grand buildings of London, right atop the dome of St. Paul's, as though crucified on the cathedral's tall cross. It glistened and glowed, then started to fall. Faster and faster it plummeted down, and made only a tiny splash in the river.

I didn't tell Mr. Goodfellow that the Stone had to be touched and coveted by another for the curse to pass on. I didn't want him to spend his last days searching for it. The Jolly Stone was better off where it was, lost in the mud of the Pool. There it might lie for all time.

Oh, I supposed a dredger might find it one day, or a mud lark might stumble upon it in a very distant year when the great river faded to a trickle. But in all likelihood the Stone had run its course, and the curse would end with Mr. Goodfellow. He had bestowed upon himself the most terrible fate of all, if little King George had told the truth. *"Those who go to their graves with the Stone unclaimed will walk the earth forever."*

I took one more look round his office, and without another word I went through his door and down to the street.

I went off in search of Midgely.

## twenty-six
## I MEET THE IMAGINARY MAN

I begged a ride on a lightering barge, along the Pool to the rusted ladder where I was sure that Calliope had borne away a frightened, shouting Midgely.

"Watch your footing!" shrieked the bargeman's wife, a husky woman.

Despite her warning I nearly came to ruin. The rungs were wet from the tide, slick with weeds, and only a timely prod from the woman's barge pole saved me from a dunking in the foul water. But I found my balance and climbed to the next rung, with the bargeman laughing behind me.

"You landsmen are like cats," he said. "All in a panic when you get your feet wet."

I ignored him. I made my way to the top of the ladder,

then down a narrow lane between two buildings. I came out in a vast space, looking up at the buildings of London and the fog that was swallowing the spires and chimneys and roofs. The new London Bridge was being built upstream from the old one, and so both river and shore were a beehive of workers. There were bricklayers with their barrows and hods, stonemasons chiseling madly, all manner of tradesmen hammering, digging, and cursing. If a building wasn't being put up, it was being torn down—like the Fishmongers' Hall, with a new one rising from the ruins of the old.

I walked to my right and turned down the first lane that I came to, only to lose myself in a maze of old warehouses. Suddenly it seemed an impossible task that lay before me, to find one little blind boy in a city that housed nearly two million souls.

Up and down I wandered; back and forth I went. I bumped into dead ends, retraced my path, and wandered round again. When I found myself back at the river, at the top of stone steps going steeply to the water, I sat down in despair.

I saw before me years and years of wandering, of searching every street, peering into every face. It was a terrible thought, for I now hated the city and longed to escape it. But I could never leave without knowing what had happened to Midgely.

I looked down a canyon between the warehouses, to row after row of rooftops. I looked the other way, up another canyon that seemed identical. I might have sat there forever, looking one way and then the other, if a little scrap of white hadn't caught my eye. It fluttered from a splintered window frame, such a useless bit of cloth that it wouldn't have meant a thing to anyone but me. Yet I knew it at once.

I got up and tore it away. I held it tightly. It was a shred of cloth that I had ripped from my own shirt long ago, one of the five lots that had been drawn in a derelict boat to see who would live and who would die.

So Midgely had hung on to those lots all this time. He must have hauled them from his pocket as Calliope hauled *him* along this very lane, and snagged one here in the hope that I would find it.

I found a second lot nearly right away, but try as I might I couldn't find a third. I went half a mile in every direction I could. I searched the ground and the walls for squirts of tobacco juice. But there was no sign that Calliope King had ever passed this way.

The fog, already, had blotted out the sun, giving evening's darkness to the day. The thought of that yellow custard pouring into these narrow spaces frightened me, and I looked up to see it oozing from the rooftops.

And there was the third lot, dangling from a bent nail well above my head. I had walked right beneath it half a dozen times.

I imagined Calliope snatching Midgely to her shoulder, hoisting him up so that she might move more quickly. I kept going along, and soon found a fourth bit of cloth hanging from the upper hinge of a green-painted door.

Here, Midge had chosen the piece that I'd marked with a knot, the one that had ruled on who would die. I took it to mean that Calliope had carried him through the doorway.

I went after them, into a deep-shadowed stillness, where the only light came through narrow windows thick with dust.

"Midgely!" I called, and a thousand pigeons rose from the floor and the rafters.

The building was one large room full of coils of rope and cable. At the front, where I'd come in, it soared to the height of a ship's topgallant, and fishing nets hung from the ceiling. At the back was a second floor, a loft that was reached by a ladder. There was a stack of paint cans, and a mountain of cork floats.

The pigeons whirred through the air, veering away from the dangling nets and the ropes. They rose in spirals from the floor to the rafters, and settled there with a mad cooing and muttering that slowly faded.

The room was so quiet then that I could hear the birds' tiny claws shuffling on the wooden beams. I smelled tarry rope and tallow, pigeons and rats and rotted wood. I heard a shuffle and rustle of some sort of animal.

The warehouse was long abandoned. The nets were so stiff with age that they might have been standing upright on their swirls and folds. They were like black columns made of rope and ancient mud, decorated with brittle shells of crab and mussel.

I took a few steps into the building. My feet slid away from me before I looked down to see the layer of bird droppings on the floor. Stamped into them was a double line of footprints, one leading away from the door, one leading back, and both vanishing into the murky gloom of the old warehouse.

I followed them warily, turning at every creak and flutter, looking all around with every step. They led me round the nets and ropes, past the mountain of cork, to the ladder that rose to the loft. Then they turned behind a stack of wooden crates, and ended at a door that was latched with a heavy bolt.

The metal screeched as I drew the bolt. The hinges must not have been oiled since Nelson's days.

Behind the door was a flight of stairs, descending to a darkness so deep that it might have had no bottom.

I stood at the top and called down, in little more than a whisper. "Midgely?"

My echo might have been someone else's voice, it sounded so timid and wary. I tried again, more forcefully. "Midge! Are you there?"

An answer came, but not in words. There was a strangled sort of groan, and a series of taps—three in a row, and three again. It stirred the pigeons on their high rafters.

I wasn't eager to go down into the darkness, but knew that I had to. I fetched a fishing cork from the big pile—it was nearly the size of a football—and used it to wedge the door open. Then I looked for a lantern, certain I would find one. Only a blind man, I thought, would use those stairs without a light.

With that, a sudden terror leapt to my mind. Down in the darkness there was not Calliope, but the old mud lark who'd wrestled me for the Jolly Stone! I was certain of it. That wordless cry had been his croaking voice. He was there in his filthy clothes, listening for me now, turning his head with that black bandage wrapped round his eyes.

The stairs trembled. My fear doubled in an instant. I imagined him crawling toward me, creeping up the stairs like a bat.

More frantic now, I searched for a lantern hung at the top of the stairs. I found a shelf—a nook—and then a candle and an old tinderbox. And I crouched on the floor, striking sparks from the flint, until the tinder glowed. I blew up a flame and got the candle going.

Its light seemed to bound down the stairs. I could see four or five steps, and not a blind man upon them. I started down, and with each stair I descended, another appeared. I tensed every muscle, expecting any instant that the blind man—or Calliope King—would come flying up at me.

Again the staircase shook. I nearly tumbled over the edge, for there was no banister to stop me. But I managed to keep my balance, and as I descended again I saw—between the steps—a person's hand holding on to the wood.

What a start that gave me! The fingers reaching from the blackness beneath the stairs, the arm stretching into it, might have belonged to a creature from my childhood nightmares. Gingerly, I crouched down and held out the candle.

A face appeared in the flickering light. It was smeared with dirt. There was a bandage covering half of it, filling the mouth. But I could see the nose and the eyes and the hair, and I knew at once I'd found Midgely.

"Oh, Midge!" I said.

I ran the rest of the way, down the stairs and around behind them. The cellar had an even greater stench of cats and rats and waste, but I paid no mind to anything except Midgely. He was tied to a post, and his hands were tied to the stairs above him. He could neither stand straight nor sit down.

How I cursed Calliope King! I couldn't believe she was as cruel as that, to leave a boy who adored her tied and gagged in a cellar. I had misjudged others, but none so badly as Calliope.

I balanced my candle on the bare earth and tore the bandage from Midgely's face. I put my arms around him and held him. "I'm sorry," I said. "Midge, I'm so sorry. I was taken away to the hulks, and—"

"It's all right. It don't matter now," said Midge. "I knew you'd come for me, Tom."

I started on the ropes that bound his hands, and all the time he kept talking.

"I've been waiting ages, ain't I Tom? But I never gave up hope. And you know something, Tom? I think you've come in the nick of time. I really do."

"Where's Calliope?" I asked as I struggled with the knots. They were good and strong; they were sailors' knots.

"I don't know where she is," said Midgely. "Did she come looking for me, Tom?"

I thought he'd gone stupid. "She snatched you from the ship. She brought you here, didn't she?"

"No," he said, in the most puzzled way.

"Then who?"

"Mr. Horrible."

The imaginary man? Now I was certain that Midge had gone off his head.

"But you know who he is, Tom?" Midgely shook his hands as they came free from the rope. He touched my shoulders and my arms. "Mr. Moyle, that's who. It was Mr. Moyle in that box the King brought aboard."

"But he drowned," I said. "How did that castaway—"

"He crawled himself to shore. That's what he told me, Tom." Midge held on to my sleeve. "He got under the dock and pulled himself along. The King and Calliope brought him aboard in that coffin."

I remembered how we'd all lent a hand to carry that thing. Calliope had persuaded us to leave it unopened.

"The King told Mr. Moyle to take me away," said Midge. " 'Hide him and wait for my word,' that's what he told him. But Mr. Moyle's tired of waiting now. He's gone to fetch his cleaver, and then he's coming back. He's going to butcher me, Tom."

*"Mr. Moyle eats children."* So Mr. Beezley had said. But I hadn't believed it then, and I didn't believe it now. "He wouldn't really do it," I said.

"Oh, yes, he would, Tom," said Midge. "We have to clear out before he comes back."

I wasn't going to argue with *that.* I thought I'd left Mr. Moyle lying drowned in a tangle of chain, and the last thing I wanted was to face him again. I went at the next set of knots in a great hurry, but Midge wasn't merely *tied* to the post; he was seized there, like a nipper to an anchor line.

I picked up the candle and started to burn through the rope. It was the old, tarry hemp from the floor above us, and a black smoke—and a smoldering flame—soon appeared. Brighter than my candle, it pushed away the blackness, and I could look farther into the cellar than I'd seen before.

In the shadows on the floor I made out the ring of a fire

pit, a circle of brick and stone. Beside it, in a little brown heap, was a frayed jacket and the sort of cloth cap that a boy might have worn. There were other things there—a black pot and white bones, and still others that didn't bear to be thought about. They made it clear to me that Mr. Beezley had spoken the truth long ago. Mr. Moyle really did eat children.

# twenty-seven

## HOW I WAITED IN THE DARKNESS

I turned away from the gruesome sights and attacked the rope with a new urgency. I twisted and pulled at the charred strands. Two of them popped apart, and a third soon after, but Midge seemed to be bound to the post as tightly as ever.

There was a burst of noise above us. In the huge room, the pigeons took flight. We heard their wings and their cooing cries, then the sound of footfalls on the floor.

"Holy jumping mother of Moses! Here he comes," said Midge.

We listened to the thumps of shoes and the creaks of wood as whoever was up there came closer. I prayed that it would be a lazy navvy shirking his job, or even a thief come prowling through the warehouse. I couldn't shake away the thought that I'd left Mr. Moyle for dead, and that if he was coming back now it would be as one of the shambling dead men who had haunted my dreams of the sea.

I turned my head to follow the sounds. The person came steadily, unerringly, toward the door at the top of the steps. I bent down and blew out my candle.

The cellar went utterly black. There was only a red glow from each parted strand of rope—six little eyes smoldering up from the ground.

"I'm coming, boy." It was Mr. Moyle. "I've brought the cleaver now."

My heart shuddered. Of all the people I'd met along my journey, Mr. Moyle was the one I feared the most. I would never forget the yellow man from Newgate, or the dying convict on Mr. Mullock's island, not the blind beggar or the bone grubber or anyone else. But Mr. Moyle was the worst.

"The little King, he played me for a fool," said Mr. Moyle in his growling voice. "Well, I'm done with waiting; it's the end for you, boy."

I held Midgely. "Don't say a word," I told him. "Don't make a sound."

The footfalls ended. There was a squelching noise from the cork I'd used to wedge the door. Then the hinges squealed, and Mr. Moyle stood at the very top of the stairs, with his shadow lying in zigzags on the steps. I listened with dread to the sound of him breathing.

"Now who is it can't close a door behind him?" he said. "Who's down there with you, boy?"

His voice was enough to give me the shivers. But his next words sent my heart leaping to my throat.

"Must be Tom Tin," he said. "Good old Tom Tin. Who else would bother with a blind boy?"

I felt Midgely tremble. I held him by the shoulders, and we waited in the darkness.

"Speak up, Tom," said Mr. Moyle. "Sing out, lad."

I peered up between the stairs. The pigeons had settled again, leaving a swirl of dust in the air. I couldn't quite see Mr. Moyle, but I could hear him breathing at the top of the steps. I saw flickers of light darting along the wall, yellow spots that flared and dimmed.

I couldn't make sense of those at first. But when I heard the sound of metal striking wood I knew what he was up to. I could see him in my mind's eye, turning and twisting the cleaver, using the blade as a reflector to light up the nooks and crannies.

I called out boldly. "Are you looking for your candle, Mr. Moyle? I've got it here."

He drew a startled breath. It pleased me that I'd surprised him.

"Blast you, boy," he said. "Well, never mind; you're no match for me."

Mr. Moyle started down the steps. The soles of his boots came into my view, then his barrel chest and the shining cleaver. Before I could move, his piglike face was there, and he saw me looking, and he laughed. "Why, there you are. Like a frightened little mouse," he said.

With that, Mr. Moyle reached back. The cork squelched, the hinges screeched, and the door slammed shut behind him. The darkness was absolute.

"We're all in the same boat now," said Mr. Moyle.

Down he came, step by step.

The only light in the whole cellar came from the glowing rope ends at my feet. They didn't cast enough glow that I could see my own shoes, let alone Midgely or Mr. Moyle. The idea that I would have to wrestle with the man in such blackness was almost more than I could bear.

The staircase was shaking. Each step took his weight with a creak and a groan.

Midgely struggled in my arms. The rope pulled and stretched, and he tried to twist away. I took a firmer hold on his shoulders, but he shouted at me. "Don't!"

Mr. Moyle stopped. "Now, now," he said. "Shouting won't do you no good. It'll all be over soon enough."

He came down another step, but where he was I didn't know. Each time he moved, a gritty shower of dust and dirt fell around me.

Midgely kept struggling. I thought he was terrified, and held him closer. In a loud whisper he said, "Let me go!"

His hands came loose. I felt him stretching the ropes, reaching toward the staircase.

Suddenly, Mr. Moyle screamed.

There was a dim, red streak as his cleaver went flying. Then he toppled forward and crashed onto the steps. He tumbled to the bottom, landing in the dirt with a thud.

"I did it, Tom," cried Midgely. "I grabbed him by his ankles, Tom."

The sounds had frightened the pigeons. I could hear nothing but the whirl of their flying. They took a long minute or more to settle again, and then the silence in the cellar was as thick as the darkness. I listened so hard that I could hear the faraway hammering from Fishmongers' Hall, and the first sad howl of a foghorn.

"He ain't moving," said Midgely. "I think he's hopped the twig."

"I hope so," I said.

"You'll have to go and look, Tom."

It scared me to leave our little hole beneath the steps. What if Mr. Moyle had crawled away while the birds were flying, and was even now creeping toward us? I picked up two of the glowing bits of rope and tried to breathe flames into the ends of them. But one went out, and then the other, the little red eyes closing, as though a small creature had just died in my hands.

"Go and look, Tom," said Midge again.

I felt my way from underneath the stairs, and down their length, until I found Mr. Moyle. My hand fell upon his trousered leg. I pushed and pulled, and it was like shaking a fat sausage. There was not a twitch of muscles, not a sign of life.

"Tom?" said Midgely.

"It's all right," I told him. "I think he's dead."

I went to the top of the stairs and opened the door. As the light spilled in, I saw Mr. Moyle crumpled in the dirt. He was sideways and crooked, lying on his chest and cheek. Scattered round his head were a few brown beads. Or so I thought at first; they were really his rotted teeth, knocked from his head by his fall.

I saw the cleaver gleaming beside the stairs. I wedged the

door again, went down and fetched it, and chopped away the ropes at Midgely's back. He nearly fell forward, but I caught him, and helped him out from under the stairs.

He said he could stand on his own. "I'm right as rain," he told me. So I let him go, rather gingerly. He went straight to Mr. Moyle, bent down, and touched the man as I had done. Then he kicked him. And he punched him. And he kicked and punched and started weeping.

"Midge," I said. I went to get him, to take him away. But he fell to his knees and kept punching Mr. Moyle.

"I hate him, Tom," he said. His little fists thumped at the man's chest. "I hate him, I hate him."

From Mr. Moyle came a groan.

To my horror, he began to move. First his fingers flexed, then his hand swept slowly out along the dirt. My first impulse was to leap away, but he was groping for his teeth!

"He ain't a goner yet!" cried Midgely. "Tom, you got to finish him off."

Mr. Moyle groaned more deeply. He gathered his broken teeth in his hand, then shoved them into his pockets.

"He'll come after us, Tom!" shouted Midgely. "Wherever we go, he'll find us. That's what he'll do, Tom. He'll hound us all our days."

I had dropped the cleaver, so I went back and got it. Midgely came along like a talking shadow. "Tom, he said he would. I told him you'd come and save me and he said it wouldn't matter. 'I'll hunt you down,' that's what he told me."

I took Midgely to the foot of the stairs, then turned him round and sent him climbing. "Wait for me up there," I said.

"Hurry Tom," he begged.

Mr. Moyle was still sprawled on the floor, trying to push himself up. I looked down at his wisps of hair, at his cheek and the side of his flattened, piggy nose. I heard Midgely crying as he tramped up the stairs.

Mr. Moyle sat upright. He was stunned and shaken—toothless now—but that was all. His eyes shifted toward me. In the darkness he wasn't much more than a shape—just a hulk of a man. But the yellow light shone in his eyes, and they seemed brimming with cunning and evil.

I threatened him with the cleaver. "If you get up, I'll kill you," I said.

"You?" He laughed. "I don't think so, boy."

A great deal of blood had bubbled from his mouth, and he wiped it away with the back of his hand. There were now only splinters of teeth sticking up from his gums, and they gave him a most vicious and ghastly appearance.

"Oh, you *want* to kill me. You'd love to kill me—but you won't," he said. "I saved your life, so you'll spare mine, because that's the proper thing to do."

"Don't wager on it, Mr. Moyle."

Up he got, unsteadily. He pressed a hand to his jaw and let out a pitiful groan. Then he stood upright, staggering sideways until he bumped against the wall.

I looked to the top of the stairs and saw Midgely vanish through the door. Now it was only myself and Mr. Moyle, and I knew that he was right. No matter what he had done, I couldn't chop him down where he stood. It wasn't because he'd saved my life in the southern seas. It was because I was not like *him*.

He was leaning against the wall, watching me with blood dripping from his mouth. "Here, give me a hand, Tom," he said. "Help me up the stairs and out to the street, then we'll be fair and square. You'll go your way, and I'll go mine."

"Good-bye, Mr. Moyle," I said.

I turned my back and went up the steps. It gave me the most dreadful shivers, for I could feel his eyes watching me, but I was determined not to seem afraid. I went steadily up, leaving him alone in the darkness.

I was two steps from the top when I heard him come flying up behind me.

I had never moved faster. I bounded to the landing; I raced through the door. I kicked away the cork and sent it bouncing off a stack of wooden crates. I heaved on the door, swinging it shut.

Mr. Moyle was halfway up, taking the stairs three at a time.

# *twenty-eight*
## OUT ON THE BEAM WITH THE BATS

The door slammed with such force that the whole building seemed to shake. It made a sound like a cannon shot, and the thousand pigeons rose as one from their perches. They wheeled and circled through the building.

I grabbed the bolt and tried to slide it through the latch. But it didn't quite meet the metal, and I had to jiggle it back and forth.

Mr. Moyle was thundering up the stairs. The pigeons were flying in frantic circles, bashing against the windows. Midgely, somewhere, was crying.

I hammered the bolt with the cleaver. I drove the tip of it into the latch.

Mr. Moyle came crashing through the door, and my cleaver went flyling.

I was thrown back against the wall, all my breath knocked out of me. Mr. Moyle staggered across the landing. He crashed into the boxes, saw the cleaver, and snatched it up. "I'll split you down the middle, Tom," he said.

I had nowhere to go but up the ladder to the loft. I sprang to the first rung and started climbing, and he came after me with the cleaver in his bloody jaws.

It was like the day long ago, when he'd chased me through the rigging of a haunted ship. I was faster now, but he was still right at my heels when I reached the top. I spilled out onto the loft and rolled away as he swung the cleaver. It chopped splinters from the wood beside me.

He was up the ladder before I could get to my feet. He pulled himself up to the floor, and I scrabbled away.

The loft was as crowded as the rest of the warehouse. It was full of rope and barrels, with only a twisting corridor between them. Mr. Moyle followed me toward the edge of the loft, where it dropped away to the floor far below.

Three pigeons went fluttering past, just above me. They veered away from Mr. Moyle, their wings and tails spreading wide, like Chinese fans. I saw the cleaver flashing at them.

I pulled myself up onto a drum of rope. Ahead of me was Mr. Moyle, thrashing his way round the pigeons. One of them had fallen, and was twitching now at his feet. Behind me was the edge of the loft, and the great beam where the nets were hung on hooks.

I stepped back onto the beam; there was nowhere else to go. Fifty feet of empty air opened below me.

The air was hot and foul here, at the very roof of the warehouse, and I saw that hordes of bats had made their home among the rafters. They clung to the wooden roof with their feet, swaying like little brown sacks. They reminded me of the close-packed hammocks of *Lachesis,* such a thickness of bats that I could scarcely see the roof. I thought, strangely, how much Mr. Mullock would enjoy the sight.

I walked backward along the beam while pigeons flew all around us. The wood was slick with the droppings of bats and birds. Mr. Moyle, with the cleaver now in his hand, was breathing his grunted breaths. His jaw was red with blood; his lips were cut and swollen.

Along the beam we went. We must have seemed two tiny figures at that great height, in all that space. With the birds wheeling around us, and the footing so poor, it was a most precarious spot. I stepped steadily back, though I couldn't see where I was going. I kept my distance from Mr. Moyle, waiting for a chance to spring at him.

It seemed that my entire journey had been for only one reason—to prepare me for this moment, to lead me to this place. My river of fate had flowed me through the proper twists and turns so that I might stand where I could not possibly have dared to stand before, with a courage I had never possessed.

I watched Mr. Moyle's feet. When they shifted forward, I moved back. When they stopped, so did I.

He swung the cleaver again. It missed me by several inches, and he followed it with a step forward. Back I went, over the hook of a hanging net.

Many of the pigeons had returned to their roosts, but

some kept flapping suddenly at our chests, as though hoping to drive us from their favorite perches. I let them flail at me with their wings, but Mr. Moyle battered them away.

We crossed half the warehouse, step by step. We crossed the mountain of cork and the heap of nets. The bats watched us with their little foxy faces. Then, right above a bare spot on the floor, I took my chance.

I waited for Mr. Moyle to swing his cleaver. It missed by barely half an inch. Then I shouted out and lunged forward.

I didn't hit the man; I didn't touch him. I couldn't take the chance that he would grab me and pull me with him. I only leapt and shouted, falling into a crouch on the narrow beam.

It was enough to startle Mr. Moyle. He flinched, and the arm that held the cleaver went high in the air to give him balance. The blade brushed through the horde of bats, and a hundred of them fell from their places.

They tumbled onto his shoulders, onto his round head. They fluttered away, or clutched on to his skin, and they let out the same strange little squeals I had heard in a faraway land. Mr. Moyle plucked two of them from his throat like hairy figs, and hurled them off. He bellowed and flailed, and the more that he moved, the more bats came down from the ceiling. They covered his shoulders and head in a twitching brown fur.

He staggered backward; he reeled sideways. The cleaver fell from his hand, spinning down toward the floor, and a moment later he followed it. With a shriek he tumbled from the beam and, still tearing at the bats, landed with a terrible sound—the crushing of bones and flesh.

There was something dreadful about bats. They were vile little things, and they could quicken the stoutest heart. If I hadn't met Mr. Mullock and his pet bat, I might have fallen from the beam that day myself. But I clung on as the creatures that Mr. Moyle had flung away went crawling across my back, across my head and my shoulders. It took a long time for all to be still and quiet again, but only then did I stand up and make my way to Midgely.

# twenty-nine
## A LAST CHAPTER

It wasn't far from the old warehouse to the docks in Limestone Reach, where my ship was waiting. Midge and I could have walked there very easily. But we had a longer errand to run, and it began at Mr. Goodfellow's office. For the fellow at the door, I produced the papers from my shirt.

He read them most quizzically, then went into the building and didn't reappear for some time. He may have talked to Silbury, or to Mr. Goodfellow himself. He didn't explain, but merely led us to the stable, where two horses stood harnessed to a curricle.

"It's yours," he said then. "Don't know why, but 'tis."

I boosted Midgely into the seat, then took my place

beside him. I shook the reins. "Get up!" I shouted at the horses. At a canter, we wheeled into the fog.

Midge was soon smiling, soon laughing, as we hurtled down the streets in this fine little rig. I turned the horses toward London Bridge, and we dashed over the Thames, above the fog-filled Pool.

It was exactly what I'd dreamed of doing, though I would never be the gentleman I'd imagined. My clothes were filthy, and the ride filled me more with fear than delight. It seemed too fast, too hurried, and the crowded streets with all their noise gave me little pleasure.

Midge hung on to the seat, reeling left and right like a little wooden boy. "Where are we now?" he asked, every two minutes.

We spent a night in a field, and arrived the next day at the hulks. Midgely, by choice, stayed in the carriage while I was rowed across the river. I climbed the long staircase to the deck of *Lachesis*. The Overseer was most surprised to see me.

"No, no, it can't be true," he said, casting glances toward the marshes. "I saw you dead and buried. Can *nothing* hold you, boy? Not my ship; not the grave?"

He was turning to shout for the guards when I told him to wait. "Read this," I said, and pushed my packet of paper into his hand.

If he was surprised before, he was flabbergasted now. But there was no arguing over the seals and signatures, and Gaskin Boggis was brought up and released from his irons. He gave me a crushing hug, and was soon giving Midgely another, when we all stood together on the riverbank.

I hadn't seen Weedle, but I'd kept my odd promise. Word of our visit would have traveled so quickly through the ship that he surely knew of it already, even as we looked out on the hulk. I crumpled his pardon into a ball and threw it out onto the Medway. It sailed away like one of Charlotte's little boats, out toward the sea.

Only a few days later we were ready to follow it, on a ship that was mine. We had a crew who sang shanties as they worked. But we had no captain then, until one stumbled along.

It was Calliope King, of course. She claimed that she just happened upon the ship, but I suspected that she'd sought it out. She must have stood on the dock for quite a while before I happened to look down from the quarterdeck.

"Hello, Tom," she called up at me. "I was starting to think I would never see you or Midgely again."

I didn't give her a warm reception. I shouted down at her, though all the stevedores were there to hear. "If you're after the Jolly Stone, you're too late. It's gone."

"Well, I'm not," she answered. "I never was."

"You knew of it?"

"I heard a tale. I didn't believe it," she shouted. "I thought it was one of Charlotte's fancies. Now, Tom, look."

I didn't want to "look." I only wanted answers to the things I couldn't explain. I leaned on the rail and shouted. "Why did you bring him aboard?"

"Who? Mr. Moyle, do you mean?" she said. "It's not easy to explain, Tom. May I come closer and tell you?"

"You may tell me from there!" I said.

"Very well." She kept looking up at me, holding back the

bits of her hair that the wind was trying to pry loose. "I wanted to bring an end to my brother's slaving business, Tom. That's what I was after. I hate every part of him, but that more than all. I thought if I could show him that I had Mr. Moyle and all the proof that I needed about his slavery, that I could stop the trade. I thought I could get justice for them both, and perhaps help you as well. That's the truth, believe it or not."

There was now quite a crowd of workers watching us. They turned their faces from Calliope to me, waiting for my answer.

"You could have explained it all straight out," I said. "Why did you sneak him aboard in a coffin?"

"Tom, I don't know," she shouted back. "Perhaps I thought you wouldn't allow me to bring him. Perhaps I thought you'd be too frightened. I really can't say. I'm a woman, after all."

There was a burst of laughter from the men. Calliope wheeled round and told them to "Stow it!" Then she looked back at me. "What more can I tell you? I don't know what happened to Mr. Moyle, or where he is, but—"

"He tried to murder Midge."

She put her hand to her mouth, and then to her heart—the very picture of surprise. But I wasn't ready to believe her innocent. "He's dead now," I said. "He's gone."

"And Midge is safe? Yes, of course he is; I see him there." She sighed, as though with relief.

"The King's dead too," I told her.

She nodded. "I know it doesn't speak kindly for me, but I didn't feel much sorrow, Tom. He could be a charming man, but what a schemer. I never trusted him."

"But you left him to look after Mr. Moyle," I said. "You were off the ship as quick as a shot, and you didn't care what happened after."

"That's not true!" she cried. "I went to see my brother. I wasn't gone more than two or three hours. Gaskin was on the ship, and Weedle too, and there was no reason to think anything would go wrong. But when I got back the ship was at the dock, and it was deserted. Utterly empty. I called for the King, but there was no answer. Even Mr. Moyle had vanished. The next morning I was told that the King had been murdered. What do you think I made of all that? Can't you imagine how I worried about Midge and you?"

At last I believed she was telling the truth. Her story matched with what I knew in every way but one. If she really returned to the ship after two or three hours, the King should still have been there. But I could imagine him hiding from her, staying silent in the dark as she searched and shouted.

"Tom, please," said Calliope. "I've been looking for you and Midge ever since. I've been haunting the river like a spirit. Is there any chance you'll forgive me?"

Midgely tugged my sleeve. I didn't know he'd come up beside me, or that he'd heard the whole exchange. "Tell her you'll forgive her, Tom, if she comes along as captain."

That was good enough for me. She came aboard that night, with a great roll of charts and a library about pilotage and the South Seas. I was amused to see among the books a copy of the very same one that had set Midgely thinking about elephant islands. And of course she brought along

Charlotte, because Midgely wouldn't have allowed for anything else.

It was hardly possible, but the girl was even more of a delight without the King around. A tiny twin of her mother, she seemed as free and wild as a rabbit in a field. I loved to see her, but it bothered me that she didn't appear to miss the King at all. "He wasn't much of a man," I said to Midgely on the day before we sailed. "But as awful as he was, he was still her father."

"No, he weren't," said Midge. "She called him daddy, but he weren't that. Her real father was a sailor what was drowned at sea when Charlotte was one year old."

We were sitting on the capstan in Limehouse Reach as the crew prepared to sail. Charlotte was setting up her tea table beside the mainmast, and the sailors had to weave around her in their work. But none minded, and all smiled.

"Calliope met the King not even two years ago," said Midge. "She put an advert in the agonies, looking for a husband so that Charlotte wouldn't have to grow up without a proper name."

Inwardly, I laughed. It seemed that every single thing the King had told me had been a lie.

"Charlotte never liked the King very much," said Midge.

"No wonder," I said. "He was such a liar and a schemer. I'm glad Charlotte's not like that. She'll always be nice."

"Maybe not, Tom. When I was little like her, I was nice too. But then I turned wicked."

"You did?" I said. There was no one less wicked than Midgely.

"Oh, yes I did," said he.

I knew that Midgely had been put on the hulk for buffing dogs, but I really had no idea what else he might have done. He grimaced now, and blushed, and I suddenly thought he was going to tell me a terrible tale.

"There was old sailors around when I was little," he said. "They'd been in the wars, and some of them had lost their arms or legs. There was some what had lost their eyes, and them blind ones sold pencils on the street. They kept their pencils in little cups."

"Yes, I know," I said.

"Well, Tom, I used to nip up and knock over them cups," said Midge. "Then I'd laugh and run away. Now that's wicked, ain't it, Tom? That's wicked through and through. I think maybe it's why I'm blinded now myself. It's payment, ain't it?"

"No, don't think like that," I said. "Midge, you're the kindest person I know."

He was certainly beloved of all aboard. His galley was already a favored place to sit and talk, and he was spending his days listening to the most stirring tales of the sea, tales that would be told over and over for him alone in the months ahead.

At the far end of the ship, Calliope appeared at the wheel. Her long dress rippled with the breeze. She looked at the shore, at our mooring lines, up to the high clouds that were flying to the east. She was smiling.

"I was stupid to think that Calliope could hurt you," I said.

"Yes, Tom, you was," said Midge.

It embarrassed me, the things I'd thought. I'd never confessed them to Calliope.

"I shouldn't have believed the King," I told Midge.

"He was a good liar."

"I even believed Mr. Goodfellow," I said. "He told me Calliope had a scheme about a ship."

"Oh, that's true, Tom. She did," said Midgely.

"What ship?"

He tapped his knuckles on the deck.

"*This* one?" I said. "You mean she was really after this ship and the diamond after all?"

"No, just the ship, Tom," said Midge.

"What was her scheme?"

He sat silent for a while, leaning against the mast. The sun was shining straight in his face, and I could see one of his eyeballs—or a part of it—gray as mud.

"What was she planning?" I asked.

"Tom, she doesn't want you to know that," said Midge. "If I tell, you have to swear I never let on."

I gave my promise, but still he hesitated. Then he touched my arm. "She wanted Mr. Goodfellow to give her the ship, or to *lend* her the ship, so she could go back to the islands and look for your father."

I was now even more ashamed. "She was trying to help me?" I said. "And I repaid her with curses?"

"Oh, she don't know if you cursed her," said Midge. "It don't matter now anyway. She's sailing the ship like she wanted, and she says you're a fine young man."

I would have asked for no better praise. I looked up at the quarterdeck, to Calliope at the wheel. Over the clamoring noise of the ship and the city, she shouted for all to hear: "Ready to cast off!" Then she looked at me. "You, there, look alive!"

Both Midge and I stood up. He turned toward the docks. "I was born here, Tom," he said. "Me mam's just over there."

It was the first time in the week we'd spent at the dock that he'd even mentioned his mother. He hadn't asked to be taken to her, or even asked *about* her.

"Why didn't you say something sooner?" I said.

"She didn't want me when she had me, Tom," he said with a shrug. "I was afraid if she saw me now she'd turf me out again. I'd rather just remember."

He went to the cookhouse, and I to the shore. The curricle I'd gotten from Mr. Goodfellow was there beside the ship. I gathered the reins and handed them to a rag picker who was passing with his barrow. "Will you hold these for me please?" I asked.

He took the reins, then watched very puzzled as I ran up the gangway to the ship. "Now look 'ere!" he called to me. "Where do you think you're going?"

"To the South Seas," I said.

"Wal-ker!" he shouted. "What do I do with this?" He held up the reins; he gestured to the carriage.

"Keep it," I said. "I've no need for it now."

We cleared the Channel on a Sunday, and bore to the south in a fresh breeze. A day or two later, clear of the land, I realized that England had vanished behind us, and the sea was empty all around. The waves were big and blue and rolling, and their white caps sparkled in the sun. Boggis was high in the foremast, and I at the wheel, and neither of us had looked back. We were both gazing ahead.

We would search for my father. I meant to look for as long as I could, and to carry him away if possible. I believed I was "doing the handsome thing." I had faced my fears and overcome them. I had made the sea my home.

# author's note

Mr. Goodfellow became a slaver by accident. He began, in my mind, only as a rich man, then became a merchant who owned ships. He lurked in my imagination for quite a while before it turned out that he transported convicts to Australia.

That was the start of it. I had to supply Mr. Goodfellow with a few ships for his business, and since I wanted them to be old and poorly maintained, I let him buy up the dregs of the slaving fleet.

Well, he got what he paid for: ships that were old and leaky, that still carried the lingering horror of their last cargos. But being Mr. Goodfellow, he didn't waste any money, or spend any time, refitting his old slavers. He put them straight into service as transports, not even bothering to remove the ringbolts where the slaves had been shackled down for the long voyage across the Atlantic. Signs of the ships' histories lay everywhere: in the forgotten lengths of rusted chain; in the stench from the bilge.

From his office in London, Mr. Goodfellow sent off loads of convicts in his miserable ships. But what would he do, I wondered, for the voyage home? He could have followed the example of the earliest convict ships, and had his own vessels carry on to India or China, where they'd collect exotic cargos to be carried home around Cape Horn, in a voyage that would circle the world. Or he could have followed the path of the transport *Boyd,* and filled his ship with timber from New Zealand. But he wouldn't have been too eager for that, as *Boyd* was attacked by Maori warriors, who killed the crew and burned the ship. Mr. Goodfellow was a man of small conscience, with ships made for slaving. His choice seemed natural; he became a slaver.

*The Castaways* is historical fiction, not a collection of facts. But I don't think it would be fair, or proper, to distort the whole history of slaving to make a story more dramatic. So the tale had to fit within the truth, rather than the other way around. Surprisingly, that wasn't so easy to sort out.

When Tom Tin tells little King George that slaving is illegal, he is right. But at the same time, he's wrong. In the time of this story, a British sea captain could be fined for carrying slaves; he could be put to death. But British landowners in the American colonies still owned slaves, and had every right to do so.

In Britain, the slave trade was outlawed in 1102, though a

sort of virtual slavery—in the feudal system—continued four hundred years, until the end of serfdom. But that didn't prevent Britons from participating in the slave trade. In 1572, John Hawkins became the first—or one of the first—English sailors to buy slaves in Africa and sell them in the West Indies. It was illegal, because he was trading with Spanish colonies, but he made enough that others followed him. Hawkins, the man who brought potatoes and tobacco to England, also launched the English slave trade.

It flourished through the 1600s, as Britain developed colonies in America. Even the King got involved, in 1660, when Charles II chartered the slaving company Royal Adventurers into Africa.

In Britain and its colonies, Englishmen owned slaves. The well-to-do put them to work as personal servants. Among these was Charles Stuart, a representative of the English government in the colony of Virginia. In 1749, Stuart bought an African slave named Somerset. Twenty years later, when his work made him travel to England, Stuart took Somerset along.

In England, Somerset went to church and was christened James. He met members of a growing antislavery movement, and in 1791, he ran away. Charles Stuart put up a reward and recaptured his slave. He imprisoned James Somerset on a ship bound for Jamaica, where Somerset would be sold and put to work on a sugar plantation. But Somerset's English godparents intervened, appealing to the courts for James Somerset to be freed. He was. The judge ruled that a slave could not be forced to leave England against his will. He did not say that slavery was illegal, or that Somerset was not a slave. But slavery was now unlawful in England, though not in the colonies.

English merchants continued to traffic in slaves. In the last half of the eighteenth century, no nation surpassed them. But opposition grew, and in 1807 Parliament passed the Abolition of the Slave Trade Act, making it an offense to transport slaves in British ships. A first step toward the end of slavery in the British Empire, it brought a tragic consequence. Faced with a fine of 100 pounds per slave, English captains began tossing their slaves overboard at the approach of a British warship. Twenty years later, the government increased the penalty. It said slaving was piracy, punishable by death.

So this is how it was at the time of Tom Tin. Throughout the Empire, in the colonies of the Americas, Britons still kept slaves. British seamen still carried slaves, but were pirates because of it. This is why Tom is both right and wrong in his opinion of slaving. It was fine to own people, just not to buy and sell them.

In 1833, Parliament passed the Slavery Abolition Act. It came into force the following year, granting emancipation to all slaves in the British Empire. For many, though, freedom didn't amount to much right away. Instead of slaves, they became apprentices, indentured to their owners. They weren't truly free for another five years, when Parliament paid a handsome compensation to the owners of plantations.

Mr. Goodfellow, of course, doesn't collect his slaves in Africa, but in Borneo and its surrounding islands in the Pacific. But, otherwise, his slave-trading operation is typical of those of the time. He is only twisting a leg of the old

"Triangle Trade" that sent ships round the Atlantic, from England to Africa, to the West Indies, and home.

It was a terrible business, where cargos of people were insured like horses and it was better for a captain to throw his slaves alive to the sea than to carry them sick to harbor. This story doesn't even touch on the awful truths of slavery. I hope it doesn't seem to make light of them.

# acknowledgments

My thanks to:

Kathleen Larkin of the Prince Rupert Library, who found the answers to many questions; Françoise Bui, my editor at Delacorte Press, who made the bad men bad, and the whole thing better; Bruce Wishart, with whom I capsized off Lucy Island, for his encouragement and help; Paul Miller, for explaining how steam engines work; David Miller, who brought a sailing doctor just when one was needed; Kristin Miller, for putting up with the sounds of writing; Jan and Goody, for lending me a name; Rick and Kim, and anyone else who followed the story of Tom Tin, for asking, What will happen next?

# about the author

Iain Lawrence studied journalism in Vancouver, British Columbia, and worked for small newspapers in the northern part of the province. He settled on the coast, living first in the port city of Prince Rupert and now on the Gulf Islands. His previous novels include the High Seas Trilogy: *The Wreckers, The Smugglers,* and *The Buccaneers;* as well as *Gemini Summer, B for Buster, Lord of the Nutcracker Men, Ghost Boy, The Lightkeeper's Daughter,* and the companions to *The Castaways: The Convicts* and *The Cannibals.*

You can find out more about Iain Lawrence at www.iainlawrence.com.